A CHOCOLATE-BOX CHRISTMAS WISH

JOSIE RIVIERA

5 STAR READER REVIEWS

Amazon Review by Book Addict:

5.0 out of 5 stars:

"I love these quick but heartfelt stories so much. Cora's story is sweet and touching, reminding us that our attitude and response to a situation are far more important than what actually occurs, and that joy is found in those tiny, ordinary moments. Whether you're short on time or not, this wholesome, inspirational holiday story is sure to lighten your heart and put a smile in your soul, so don't miss it."

Amazon Review by Aunt Sis:

5.0 out of 5 stars:

I especially like reading about women whose father taught them about cars, especially jumper cables and how to change a tire!"

Amazon Review by Jude's Books:

5.0 out of 5 stars:

"This book is Cora's story, I liked her and was delighted to read about her. It was a very good read.

Josie is an experienced, gifted author.
I would recommend this book to you."

INTRODUCTION

To keep up on newly released ebooks, paperbacks, Large Print Paperbacks, audiobooks, as well as exclusive sales, sign up for Josie's Newsletter today.

As a thank you, I'll send you a Free PDF ... The Beauty Of ...

Josie's Newsletter

Did you know that according to a Yale University study, people who read books live longer?

This book is dedicated to all my wonderful readers who have
supported me every inch of the way.
THANK YOU!

PRAISE AND AWARDS

USA TODAY bestselling author

CHAPTER ONE

*H*igh on a rain-drenched hill, Cora Carpenter set down her mug of tea and stared out the kitchen window of her bungalow. The stream of chatter from the children in her day care had ceased, leaving the quiet of a cloudy California afternoon.

She didn't focus on Evanville's town square below, which she easily spotted from her window. Soon, the square would boast hundreds of twinkling white lights as night fell. Or, if she opened her window, the faint sounds of a community concert might drift up to her.

The window remained closed, the concert quiet, because one weekly chore pervaded her thoughts. She dreaded grocery shopping on Thursdays. And today was Thursday.

Never much of a cook she found preparing a spread for a single person, namely herself, was disheartening. Not to mention it emphasized she was alone, without anyone to share meals or companionship.

She blew out a sigh. So?

So, it was no big deal, right?

Wrong.

Perhaps it was society's lofty expectations. Every television commercial promoted sharing holiday festivities with a partner.

Not her, though. She wouldn't expose herself to the hurt that inevitably followed.

She turned as Jack, her brother, breezed into the kitchen. Bald, sporting a thin black mustache, and older than she by a decade, he told everyone he was a confirmed bachelor.

"Smells good in here." He made a beeline for the cinnamon cookies on the counter. "Are you holiday baking, already?"

"Cinnamon and cream cheese are key ingredients." She gestured to the trays. "Try one."

"Only one?" He snatched a handful.

"Or take a dozen. A couple of the older children and I baked them for you and the nurses at the hospital."

"Much appreciated." He craned his neck to peer out the window. "By the way, Evanville pulled out all the stops for the holidays, complete with a strolling Christmas tree."

"I don't remember anyone mentioning a strolling tree," Cora said.

"It's an innovative idea by the town council's think tank."

"*Our* town council has a think tank?"

He winked between bites. "More like the mayor and his wife. You'll notice the tree when you visit downtown."

"How ... jolly." She lifted a snowman mug to her lips and gave her reindeer earrings a toss. "What's more festive than a walking tree?"

"A *strolling* tree," he corrected. "And, there's something even more exciting."

"The live nativity?"

"The annual *candy-cane-eating contest*." Dramatically, he enunciated every word.

"A favorite of yours because you've won three years in a row." When he didn't reply, she asked, "Are you entering?"

"I probably should give other people a chance." He sported a smug grin. "But I won't. Besides, all the extra sugar in candy canes leads to only one result."

"Which is?"

He poured a mug of coffee for himself. "Obesity."

Despite herself, Cora laughed at her brother's good humor, his acceptance of himself as an overweight man. Lighthearted, embracing the comedy in life, he pushed away the loneliness in her chest.

"Are you participating in the hospital's 5K charity run?" he asked.

She smoothed her khaki-colored sweatshirt, embroidered with the likeness of a cherry-red cardinal. "Sadly, I'm out of shape."

"You're lanky and lean. Me, on the other hand ..." He patted his protruding stomach. At six feet and three hundred pounds, Jack was at a weight many people, including his doctor, labeled as morbidly obese.

"The run is important to me," he went on, "because it benefits Project Nutrition." He grabbed a napkin to wipe his mouth and tossed it in the trash. "Needless to say, I'll be walking."

"I read about the program," Cora replied. "They implement cost-effective strategies, such as adding iron to food to help cut childhood anemia."

"Malnutrition contributes to a number of developmental delays." As always, Jack spoke passionately when talking about kids. He was a nurse in the children's ward at the local hospital. Both he and Cora had chosen child-oriented occupations, and they loved youngsters, although neither of them were married nor had children.

He set down his mug and picked up a paper and pen.

"Are you taking notes on how many candy canes you're required to devour in order to win the contest?" Cora joked.

"Nope. I already know."

"How many?"

He zipped his lips with his fingers.

She chuckled at the image of a secretive Jack sitting at a table piled high with candy canes in the festively decorated town square.

"I'm an organized person and preparing my holiday shopping list," he said.

"Right now?"

"Why not?" Sheepishly, he grinned. "What's your Christmas wish this year, Cora?"

She tapped her fingers on the counter. "I can't think of anything special."

"December twenty-fifth isn't far away. You must have an idea."

"Honestly, I don't." She squinted at the paper as he quickly jotted numbers. "What are you writing?"

"My ideal weight." He presented a guilty smile and set the pen down. "And have you decided whether you'll fly to Nevada with me to visit Mom?"

"Maybe."

He let out a frustrated sigh. "That's not an answer."

Cora turned and began wrapping the cookies for him to take with him. She exhaled, only then recognizing she'd been holding her breath.

In truth, she'd made her choice. Their mother, Zoe, had raved for weeks about her latest beau, and Cora suspected that adult children would be in the way of this fresh romance. Their visit might result in an awkward situation.

Jack, apparently, harbored no such qualms.

"Well?" He counted off the days on his fingers until Christmas.

"I'll stay in town," Cora replied. "If any of my child-care parents are working extra shifts, they'll call for me to watch their kids."

"You deserve a week off."

"I want to be available just in case, but will plan to take time off between Christmas and New Year's." She provided a small smile. "We'll agree on a raincheck for me to visit Mom, okay?"

"Don't you want to accompany me on my first solo flight?"

She stiffened. "You're flying a plane yourself?"

"A commuter plane. I finally earned my pilot's license, and it's an hour flight from California to Nevada." At Cora's frown, he smiled reassuringly. "My instructor offered to fly with me."

"Olivia?" Cora's mind raced with the possibilities. "The woman with curly auburn hair down to her waist who recently graduated from college?"

"One and the same. After sixty hours of flight time, thirty of flight briefings, and forty hours of ground school, I'm ready."

"To date or to fly?"

"Both." He hooked an arm around her waist and twirled her, singing "I'll be Home For Christmas."

Laughing, she leaned against the counter to shake off the dizziness. "Are you abandoning bachelorhood for a woman fifteen years your junior?"

"Me? A man who prizes my unmarried status?" He looked out the window again and cleared his throat. "Have you spoken to Dad? I realize you might still be angry at him, what with his tendency to try to control our lives."

"*Tendency* to control?"

"Yeah, more than a tendency." Jack gave a quick laugh. "Well, have you?"

"I've reached out to him."

She chewed her bottom lip. She had no desire to revisit *that* argument. Her father's vocal opinions had left her panicked and embarrassed. In short, he'd been opposed to her dating the man she'd met online because he believed he was a con. She'd refused to listen. Her father had never liked any of the men she'd dated.

Then he'd chided her for being a silly, desperate fool, and they had quarreled. Wasn't it her decision as a grown woman to date whoever she pleased?

Besides, she wasn't desperate. Was she?

Mentally, she reviewed her childhood. Her father had always criticized her, especially after he and her mother had divorced. Don't wear revealing clothes, don't attend any university except the one he selected. His overbearing demands of how she should behave had become the thread mark of their conversations.

Now she was sorry for the argument because she'd raised her voice to her own father. He'd been right.

She swallowed the lump in her throat.

Weren't most decisions easier in hindsight?

"Don't be offended by Dad's outburst." Jack retrieved a worn teddy bear from the floor and deposited it in a plastic bin. "Refuse to let a scam artist ruin your Christmas."

She accepted Jack's words in the vein they were meant— encouragement from a caring older brother. Thankfully, he didn't press her for more details.

"So what's your wish?" he repeated.

She surveyed the kitchen—the cabinets that hadn't been painted in a decade, the leaky sink faucet, the budget-friendly linoleum.

Grimacing, she finally said, "I'd love a bright and shiny stainless-steel refrigerator."

He chuckled. "A refrigerator is not a Christmas wish."

"When it's twenty years old and formerly belonged to our

parents, then it constitutes a wish." She nodded to the pen. "Write that down."

"Mom and Dad split long ago, and you can't break up with your refrigerator." He pinned her with a thoughtful gaze. "Think of something else."

"A dishwasher to replace the one I never had?"

He tapped his foot and snatched another cookie before she could to wrap it. "Nope."

"A shelving unit for baby board books?" She stepped into the living room. "Better yet, a chest full of educational toys."

"I meant a special wish for you." Jack peered at the wall clock. "My hospital shift begins at three. Keep thinking and we'll talk soon, okay?"

"Okay. I'm off to complete my least favorite task."

"Grocery shopping?"

"You know me well." She pushed a strand of hair from her face. She didn't fuss with her appearance. She'd always preferred to style her dark hair in a short pixie cut, but lately had let it grow out. Who had hours for fancy grooming while watching youngsters all day?

Jack placed his mug in the sink. "You'll stop at Olive's Diner first?"

"I'm a creature of habit." She shook her ponytail free and dug through her purse for the key to her ten-year-old Chevy. "A meal at the diner definitely brightens my Thursdays."

On the drive to town, she mulled over Jack's Christmas-wish question and chided herself on her responses. Instead of materialistic or self-centered items, she should wish for something that benefitted others.

Her mind wandered, taking inventory of her to-do list:

Home decorating, gift-giving, writing out cards, baking ...

Once, she'd treasured the Christmas holiday. The days

were thrilling, not demanding. Lately, endless activities screamed to be accomplished. What did it all mean, the frantic rush to accomplish everything by New Year's? Was it acceptable to think of herself?

She switched on her car radio, and the melodic strains of "A Holly Jolly Christmas" came through the speakers. Would she ever reach a place when the holidays didn't retell what had vanished from her life?

She'd believed that Gregory Pansa loved her, and they would spend Christmas together on the beach in Florida. He'd promised. Unfortunately, he never existed.

Burl Ives continued crooning about the best time of the year, and Cora sang along. One constant hadn't changed.

Her love of music.

*T*hirty minutes later, Cora sat at her preferred booth in Olive's Diner, enticed by the scents of buttery mashed potatoes and a pot roast simmering with root vegetables. Comfort-foods, timeless and hearty staples.

She rotated a string of Christmas oldies in the jukebox every week while she ate.

Today was no exception, and she fed the jukebox enough coins so that Elvis Presley repeatedly belted out a tune about his blue Christmas.

Oliver, the owner and an amiable man in his thirties, stepped to the booth and poured her a cup of coffee. "How are the peanut butter cups?" he asked.

She touched her hands to her lips. "Delicious, as always. An ideal end to a wonderful meal."

"Thanks to Sally." The pride in his tone was apparent. "It's her recipe."

"Yes, so you've mentioned." *A million times.*

Oliver's hazelnut eyes lit with warmth whenever he

mentioned Sally Elliot. They'd met the previous Valentine's Day when she and several other customers had been stranded at his diner because of a violent storm. She was a chocolatier and owned a candy shop in Bloomingfield, a couple hours' drive from the diner. Sally and Oliver had created the recipe that night.

"I can't make these peanut butter cups fast enough," he said. "Every Thursday, I place two aside for you."

"I admire your thoughtfulness." Cora unwrapped the second candy on her plate. "Have you and Sally planned a wedding date yet?"

"February fourteenth. Her daughter, Clarissa, will be our flower girl."

His ecstatic expression prompted Cora's smile. "Is Sally aware of your plans?"

"Not yet." A wide grin split his face. "I'm surprising her with an engagement ring on Christmas day, and a Valentine wedding is—"

"Romantic." Cora clasped her hands together. The thrill of the romance brought goose bumps to her arms. "Let me add *brilliant* and *delightful*."

"I show my love on my sleeve, don't I? When it comes to Sally, I'm definitely starry-eyed."

"Don't ever change, Oliver." Despite her encouraging smile, Cora bit back a resigned sigh. When had she last experienced any of those wonderful emotions called love?

She hadn't.

That is, not until she recently met a man on an online dating platform. On a whim, she'd joined the site and uploaded her profile and picture. The man's photo displayed a middle-aged, black-bearded guy in medical scrubs by the name of Gregory Pansa.

Soon after, he'd messaged her. He was a doctor who lived in Egypt, trying desperately to return to America because he was a US citizen. Day after day he endured one obstacle after another. He was out of money because his funds were tied up in a foreign bank account, he'd been in an accident and was in the hospital. Or, the latest, he'd missed his flight to the States.

At first, she had shaken her head in exasperation. But the more he emailed, the more she believed him. Surely he wasn't scamming her, no matter what her father contended.

Not now. Not during the holidays.

Gregory complimented her "soulful amber eyes rimmed by generous black lashes" and her "velvety-smooth complexion." She embraced his poetic words since they brought a rush of exhilaration. Perhaps Gregory was *the one*.

Her father investigated further, drawing her attention to numerous inconsistencies with Gregory's story. Finally, she faced the fact that Gregory Pansa wasn't real.

She'd been a fool. Plus, she was out two thousand dollars.

She sank back in the booth and allowed Elvis Presley's deep voice to carry a note of warmth into a chilly afternoon.

The diner's door swung open and a tall man filled the entrance with his broad shoulders and strong frame. His handsome, sun-kissed face set in a mild frown while he surveyed the diner. Quickly, he strode to the counter as Oliver emerged from the kitchen carrying a tray of red velvet cakes.

Cora turned to watch their exchange. Customer chats around her table stilted.

"Is there a garage nearby?" the man inquired. "My car broke down a mile from here."

Oliver set down the tray. "Were you in a car wreck? Are you all right?"

"No. I'm fine."

"You walked?"

"It isn't far."

"Far enough. Fortunately, the rain never started."

"Right." Grimly, the man looked toward the window, then at Oliver. "Are you the cook?"

Oliver gave a slight bow. "I'm the owner. Oliver."

"Patrick Gervez." The man removed his black leather gloves, shoved them into the pockets of his tan wool coat, and the men shook hands. "I'm on my way to Bloomingfield."

"You're new here?" Oliver asked.

"Brand new. Actually, I was aware of the forecast because Lorenzo Rossi, the meteorologist, called to inform me. I'll be working with him, and he wanted to make certain I arrived in Bloomingfield safely."

"Where are you from?" Oliver set the plated cakes in the bakery case. "California drivers aren't recognized for their competency on wet roads, and we catch plenty of rain in winter."

"I'm off the hook then. I'm relocating from Raleigh, North Carolina."

"Raleigh is a sizable city."

The man pressed his lips together. "Yep."

"And Bloomingfield is a modest town." Slowly, a smile dawned across Oliver's face. "My fiancée, Sally, mentioned you, Patrick. Lorenzo married her sister, Julie."

"I heard." Patrick shifted. "The garage?"

"Harry's Car and Truck Service is open from early morning till about four, so it might be too late. I'll call, just to be certain." Oliver reached for his cellphone.

As Cora and the other patrons looked on, Oliver's unanswered call confirmed that Harry's Garage was clearly closed.

At Patrick's frustrated groan, Oliver signaled to Cora. He didn't need to say anything because she immediately realized what he requested.

She grabbed her purse and hurried to the counter. "I can help you, Patrick," she offered.

Patrick glanced at her. "A pair of jumper cables are called for, miss. Thanks, anyway." He considered Oliver. "Do you have any?"

"Nope," Oliver replied.

"I do," Cora piped in. "I keep jumper cables in my car."

Patrick's dark eyebrows raised. He rubbed the slight beard on his chin. "You do?"

"Doesn't everyone?"

A corner of his full mouth turned up in a self-deprecating smile. "Apparently, I don't."

She gazed into his intense blue eyes and managed a straight face. "Well, the penalty for not being prepared is—"

He bent and whispered in her ear, "A Christmas angel floated to my rescue exactly when I needed her."

His words brought a flush of warmth to her cheeks, and she drew back. The trace of his aftershave, a mild pine scent, filled her nostrils. Clean and heady, bringing to mind a woodsy outdoor fire.

Her hands fluttered. A sidelong glance at a grinning Oliver reminded he was ever the romantic. She sent him a glare, silently stating, *Get that smirk off your face.*

"I'm hardly an angel," she replied to Patrick. "I store jumper cables in my trunk, along with a first aid kit and a flashlight in the glove compartment."

"I like a woman who is always prepared. I'm obviously failing in that department and—" From his expression, he grimly rebuked himself.

She held up a hand before he finished. "You can't antici-pate when an emergency will happen." He was easily over six feet tall, a giant compared to her under five feet height. Better responses flooded her brain, but she shifted back to him. "Incidentally, did you shut your car's engine off?"

"I didn't have a choice. The car stalled."

"Does it stall a lot?"

"More and more."

"Then the damage to your battery is already done." She extended a smile. "I'll drive you to your car, and the jumpstart should get you on the road to a service station."

"Will I reach Bloomingfield?"

"You should."

"Should?"

"Barring any unforeseen circumstances."

"Like what?"

"A flat tire."

"Thanks, that's reassuring." He didn't appear pleased at her statement, although he held out his hand. "I'm Patrick Gervez."

"I overheard." She stretched out her hand to his. "In Olive's Diner, everyone makes it a point to know everyone else's business."

"I see," Patrick wryly observed. "And you are ...?"

"Cora Allbright."

His fingers were firm, yet warm and gentle, and an unanticipated jolt of attraction sent a fluttering sensation straight through her pulse.

Quickly, she drew her hand away.

"I'm pleased to meet you, Mrs. ...." he began.

"It's miss and call me Cora."

He considered her with a smile of open, male interest, so flattering and unsettling that she focused on standing still, fearful of stumbling if she took more than a step.

He tipped his head. "Cora is a beautiful name."

"Thanks." She straightened and gazed up at his outrageously good-looking face. "A pleasure, Mr. Gervez."

"Patrick. I'm new to California."

"I've lived here all my life."

"And you're the first person I've met, aside from Oliver."

"Lucky you," she joked.

"Nice earrings." He drew attention to the miniature reindeers swinging from her ears.

"They glow. Their noses—"

"Like Rudolph."

"Correct."

They shared a smile.

*M*inutes later, with Patrick in the passenger seat of her Chevy, Cora stopped in front of his stranded car on the side of the road. He might be new to the area, she reflected, but his car was the opposite.

He insisted on her waiting while he scurried around to open the door for her. Although their fingers hardly touched as she got out, her hand tingled. Determined to ignore her reaction, she stroked his classic Mustang's shiny navy-blue exterior. "This is gorgeous. You drive a sleek convertible."

"Do you like it?"

"A Mustang? Definitely."

"So do I, when it runs. Usually, the car is reliable."

She grabbed her jumper cables from her trunk. "You traveled all the way from the Carolinas?"

"A four-day drive that took thirty-nine hours. My Mustang never disappoints. Until this afternoon, that is."

She lifted the hood, grateful she'd dressed casually in dark-washed jeans and the comfortable jean jacket she'd donned over her sweatshirt.

"My father was a mechanic and taught me and my brother everything," she said. "In fact, my father has a weakness for older cars, much like me."

Patrick gave a thumbs-up. "We share a commonality, except all I know about cars is I want them to run."

She chuckled.

"Your father sounds highly competent," Patrick said.

"He is." And she loved her father, their recent argument notwithstanding. She'd phoned to apologize, but he hadn't picked up nor responded to her voice mails.

Patrick studied her. "Are you close?"

"Why do you ask?"

"By the expression on your face, he must mean a great deal to you."

"He's one of the most important people in my life." She walked to her car to prop the hood, aware of his gaze on her back. If she chatted with him any longer, she might divulge the entire, sad story of her failed online dating and the ensuing fight that had severed any last rapport with her father.

Patrick yanked off his coat and placed it in his car. "How can I help, Cora?"

"I'm all set, and this won't take long." Explaining the process, she fastened the clamp on the red jumper cable to her car's battery, and the other red clamp to the positive terminal on Patrick's car and then the black clip to Patrick's negative terminal and to her own car's unpainted metal surface—not near the battery.

"Very impressive," he murmured. "Thank you."

"You're welcome. Wait for a while so my engine can charge your battery." She slid into the driver's seat of her car, lowered the window, and gestured for Patrick to do the same. "Try starting it now," she called.

He spun the ignition and the engine immediately purred to life. "Wow." He applauded. "You're a wizard."

"Hardly, but thanks."

He strode to her car and bent down to peer at her through the open window. "If I were you, I'd ask me out to dinner to offer my appreciation."

"What?" She blinked. Startled laughter bubbled to the surface. "Say that again?"

"I wanted to get your attention." A grin tugged at his mouth. "Will Saturday evening suit you?"

Somehow, she kept her expression noncommittal. "I can't."

"Why not?"

"I'm ... I'm cleaning my refrigerator, but thank you for the invitation."

"Is Sunday night better?"

"I'm considering running a 5K and should practice ... running."

"You can advise me on the necessary emergency equipment to store in my trunk while we dine."

"No. Sorry."

"I hoped chatting about cars might attract you."

It did. Spending time with him attracted her even more.

She brought her thoughts back to reality and shifted her attention to the road. "I'm on a dating hiatus."

"Why? A bad breakup?"

Briefly, she nodded.

"When did your hiatus begin?" He brushed a hand across his forehead as a slight drizzle began falling.

"Last month."

"Mine is three years, so I've got you beat." He leaned in. His scent again, a whiff of pine and infinitely appealing.

"I guess you're the winner," she replied.

"Have you heard the phrase, 'a tincture of time'?"

"You mean, 'time heals all wounds'?"

"'A tincture of time refers more to bodily ailments." His voice was deep and entirely too certain. "Whereas 'time heals all wounds' indicates time's healing nature."

"It depends on how you define the word *heal*."

"In time, you will heal." He straightened. "Look, I really appreciate you helping me. You lost an hour of your afternoon around helping me."

"It's not a loss. I'm happy to assist."

"Few people extend themselves nowadays."

"You'll discover things are different here."

A spark of pleasure lit his features. "Highly reassuring. Big cities are often uncaring, you know?"

She didn't know. She'd never lived anywhere else—always residing in the tiny town of Evanville, where everyone knew each other by name.

She lifted her face to his and her heart skipped a beat. His brown hair was thick and wavy and a tad too long, his eyes a piercing blue. He'd folded his white shirtsleeves up on his powerful forearms when he offered to help her with the jumper cables, and the masculinity he exuded left her breathless.

And here, on this wet December day, she felt an instant magnetism to a man she just met. She hadn't expected that and wondered if her fair skin concealed the telltale flush of awareness heating her cheeks.

At his perceptive smile, she highly doubted it.

"Where do you work?" An unruly lock fell onto his forehead, damp with the drizzling rain. His hair was naturally wavy, and she resisted the urge to brush it back.

Don't you dare, she reprimanded herself. The gesture would be much too familiar.

"I run a licensed child care from my home," she responded.

"I've heard licensing isn't an easy process."

"Where did you hear that?"

"My wife, I mean my ex-wife, Olympia, and I interviewed numerous daycares. In the end, Olympia decided she didn't want children after all. Her decision, not mine."

So he'd been married and divorced.

"I take my role seriously," Cora replied. "I'm responsible for the health and safety of the kids I watch."

"All ages?"

"Preschoolers in the morning and school-age in the afternoon."

"I suspect you're a wonderful caregiver."

He assessed her with those gorgeous eyes. Up close, specks of gold enhanced the vivid blueness.

"I love children," she said.

"I do too."

For several beats he was silent. His shuttered expression revealed there was more, but it was swiftly replaced with a charismatic smile.

Everyone had a story and oftentimes, a haunted past. She debated. She didn't know him well, but went with her gut instinct. "If you ever choose to talk—"

"About what?"

"Life, children, failed relationships ..." *Had she really suggested that?*

"No. I won't." His gaze swung from hers. "Thanks for the offer, though."

Normally, fine-looking men didn't interest her. In her limited experience, they were generally self-centered. Patrick seemed considerate, genuinely attentive and appreciative.

Stylish, high-profile women probably fell into his arms if he showed the slightest interest.

Cora, though, was neither stylish nor high-profile, and for once she was pleased with her flaws. That way, he wouldn't be interested enough to bring on the full potency of his magnetic appeal.

Belatedly realizing she'd studied him far too long, she blurted, "I've worked from home the past few years."

"You're an entrepreneur. Another admirable trait besides being a beautiful car mechanic." His gaze drifted to her face. "Before I leave, shall I try to ask you out again?"

She shot him an expression of tolerant amusement and shook her head.

"You're getting wet," she pointed out.

"Well, then, I should go." He glanced at his watch. "I anticipate seeing you around."

Around? Around where? And what about his dinner invitation? Had he accepted no for an answer so easily?

He'd asked twice. She'd refused twice.

"Sure," she muttered. "Let me unhitch our cars."

She removed the jumper cables and recommended he purchase a new battery immediately. "Good luck on your move," she said as they each got back into their cars.

As he drove off, she reassured herself he had wreaked enough havoc on her for one afternoon. It was probably for the best if they didn't meet again.

She'd felt an instant, powerful draw to him that he apparently ... didn't feel for her.

She braced her palms on the dashboard and collected a slow, steady breath. Hadn't she learned from painful experience that she was a terrible judge of men?

Nonetheless, the idea of dining with Patrick, sitting across from him in a restaurant as he gazed at her, being held in his arms while he kissed her ... Listening to the community band in the town square, the charm of miniature white lights glowing from boutiques while they strolled through picturesque towns, the creation of Christmas memories ...

Nope. Not going there.

Her encounter with Patrick was happenstance, her daydreams nothing more than fantasies. With that, she forced any further contemplations of him from her mind.

CHAPTER TWO

*F*our days later, Cora and her part-time employee, Molly, spent an early evening cleaning and straightening Cora's living room. Her home was licensed for up to six children, and they all had appeared at dawn.

Now they had departed with their parents, and only two weeks remained until Christmas.

Cora plucked the dead leaves from a pink poinsettia plant a parent had gifted her and arranged it on a side table.

Finished with her tasks, Molly walked into the kitchen. She perched on a stool, her fingers rapidly texting, when Cora entered.

"How did you spend your weekend?" Molly's attempt to disguise a grin failed.

"I jogged on Saturday and Sunday to get in shape for the hospital's charity run."

"Did you have any interesting romantic adventures?"

Cora set down a toy truck she held. "Why do you ask?"

"Because Harry texted me." Molly cut her gaze to her cellphone. "He heard you met a guy in Olive's Diner."

"Who told him?"

"Oliver. He mentioned he had called Harry's garage on Thursday to help a new guy in town because his car had broken down, and you came to his rescue."

"Cars are my specialty." Cora pasted on a bright smile. "The guy owns a gorgeous Mustang."

"Uh huh." Deliberately, Molly set her cellphone to the side. "I wonder who he is?"

"His name is Patrick, and he's relocating to the Bloomingfield area."

"Uh-huh."

"What's with all the 'uh-huh's'?" Idly, Cora spun the tiny wheels of the truck, recalling her racing pulse when she was around Patrick. Flattered he asked her out to dinner, she also feared becoming nothing more than a conquest if she spent another minute with him.

"Why is he in this quiet part of California?" Molly asked.

Cora shrugged. "He's going to work with Lorenzo Rossi. Perhaps he's a newly hired cameraman for the TV station."

"Is he single?"

"Yes. He's divorced." Cora climbed onto the stool across from Molly. "He requested I go on a Saturday night dinner date with him."

"You certainly brightened my Monday." Molly leaned forward. "Ditch the clothes you normally wear that are a size too big and show off the lovely figure you always hide."

"I can't wear tight outfits and high heels running around after children all day."

"But you can on a date with a guy who's got excellent taste in cars. When are you going?"

Molly had been married a year, and assumed everyone should be in a constant, blissful, newlywed state consisting of flowery words and endless kisses. The Christmas season merely heightened her enthusiasm.

"No date." Cora rubbed her neck. "We're not, because—"

"I realize you're in a once-bitten-three-times-shy frame of mind. Don't let that prevent you from pursuing a good life."

"Once bitten, twice shy," Cora corrected. "And thanks for the unsolicited opinion, Ann Landers."

"Who's she?"

Cora offered a bemused grin. "An advice columnist, evidently before your time."

"Move forward and begin real live dating, like your father advised. Have you settled your differences with him?"

Cora vacantly fixed her gaze on the Santa's Village cookie jar on the counter, and didn't reply.

"Forget the online Egyptian stuff," Molly said firmly.

Molly knew about the fictional Gregory Pansa, and the general string of bad luck Cora had experienced with boyfriends. Prior to Gregory, she'd dated infrequently. Nothing had worked out, although she invariably chose to be fair and allow the men a chance. In most cases, her instincts had shouted *no*, but she hadn't listened.

Her instincts had been right on. No man had appealed to her.

And she'd been the biggest chump of all. Even when her father had hired a private investigator, and it turned out that Gregory wasn't a doctor living in a church basement in Egypt —a church that incidentally didn't exist—Cora hadn't accepted the fact that the romance was a hoax.

"Enough about my nonexistent dating life." Dismissively, she flapped her hand, hoping Molly got the hint and dropped the subject of Patrick. "My brother wants me to make a Christmas wish. Any suggestions?"

"Well, duh." Molly drew a laughing breath. "How about a new man? Someone honest, reliable and handsome. Looks aren't all that important, but while we're wishing ..." She included a whimsical sigh.

Cora stood and dragged the vacuum cleaner from the hall

closet, intending to vacuum the carpet, the final chore for the day. When she switched it on, sparks flew through the air.

With a last spurted cough, it died.

"There's my wish." Cora half-laughed. "A brand-new vacuum cleaner."

*A*fter Molly left, Cora settled on the plaid sofa in her living room and reached for a cup of green tea. The local broadcast was televised every evening, and she took an active interest in the latest news, weather and local sports updates.

She knew Lorenzo, the meteorologist, and appreciated his witty forecasts. Straightaway, he dove into his habit of changing a dismal forecast into a funny, upbeat occurrence.

"Clouds are still hiding our California sun, and precipitation is producing the ideal climate for ducks." He gestured to the weather screen showing rain clouds, then opened an umbrella and whistled the refrain from "Singin' in the Rain." He even twirled.

She laughed out loud. Perhaps she'd contact Lorenzo and inquire about Patrick ...

What? No. She refused to chase after a man she'd met in a diner. Especially one who'd requested she have dinner with him not once but twice, then hadn't seemed interested after all.

A new anchorman was introduced during the next segment, and Patrick Gervez's handsome face appeared on the television screen.

A tentative smile formed on Cora's lips as surprise kicked in.

Patrick was the new anchor? Not a cameraman?

She remained glued to the entire broadcast, entertained by the clever banter between him and the various announcers.

When Lorenzo returned, he concluded his segment singing "White Christmas," performed with a pair of sleigh bells as accompaniment.

"So, Lorenzo, you're overflowing with props and tunes tonight." Patrick folded his hands on the news desk. "Shall I harmonize?"

"I'm content singing solo." Lorenzo launched into a tuneful "I'm Dreaming of a ..."

Cora made the mistake of focusing on Patrick, and noticed the crinkles around his blue eyes, which were perilously appealing when he laughed.

"Lorenzo," he said, "Speaking of holiday tunes, will you enlighten us on the story behind 'Jingle Bells'?"

"The song was published in 1857, right around the year when you were born," Lorenzo joked.

Patrick grinned. "Did you know it was the first song transmitted from space?"

"I know now." Lorenzo strode to the anchor desk and took a seat beside Patrick.

"As our viewers are aware, I'm new to the area," Patrick continued. "Lorenzo, what can you tell me about Bloomingfield?"

"It's the quintessential small town."

"Have you lived here your entire life?"

"Not yet."

At Patrick's chuckle, Lorenzo countered, "Any final words to end your first broadcast?"

Patrick's eyebrows furrowed while he gave the question serious deliberation. His eyes sparkled and a mysterious smile edged his lips. "I'm pleased to be a part of this award-winning station and now residing in this lovely new town."

There was that word, new, Cora thought, as she squeezed a slice of fresh lemon into her tea. All references regarding Patrick seemed to circle back to that word.

"Everyone I've met this week has been friendly and help-ful." He paused, staring directly into the camera. "I particu-larly want to thank a woman named Cora, who braved the rain to fix my temperamental car."

Cora? He was referring to her? On live television?

Dumbfounded, Cora almost dropped her cup. Hastily, she placed it on the coffee table.

Her cellphone rang. When she picked up, Molly demanded, "Is the dreamboat newscaster who just went off the air your Patrick?"

Cora visualized Molly's self-satisfied grin.

Although filled with joy, she refuted, "He's not *my* Patrick. We just met."

"Well, he's definitely not *my* Patrick. I'm married to Harry, and together we'll dash through the snow in a ten-horse open sleigh."

Cora chuckled, not bothering to correct Molly. She peered out the window, the dark sidewalks illuminated by the colored holiday lights of her neighbors' homes. "What snow?"

"I'm quoting the lyrics to a song."

Well, not exactly. Cora put her head in her hands and sighed.

Molly laughed, then dipped her voice to an amplified whisper. "The woman he referred to was you, correct?"

Cora nodded into the phone. When she clicked off, it immediately rang again.

And again.

First Jack, then Oliver, shadowed by her mother, who Jack had apparently alerted.

As Cora readied for bed, another *new* floated through her mind.

Perhaps she should get a *new* phone number.

CHAPTER THREE

The week passed and Cora fended off suggestions from her friends, mother, and brother that she should contact Patrick.

"I'm too busy," she rationalized. "Besides, it's Christmastime."

Which was true. Plus, the kids in her care were in hyper mode. Consequently, she and Molly were exhausted at day's end.

Furthermore, Cora hadn't begun any holiday decorating. Inside, decorating meant setting up a miniature pine tree in the living room, and adding ornaments of the children around the branches.

The outside, though, was a different matter.

On Tuesday evening, she discovered that half the multicolored icicle lights for her porch railings didn't work, and opted to string clear lights, instead. A twinkle of cheer was exactly what her bungalow lacked, and she anticipated the smiles on the children's faces when they dashed up to her house.

Sparkly, bright and ...

Her mind swung to Patrick.

New.

The next morning, she requested that each child bring in a cookie recipe for a reception on December 23, the day before she officially closed for the holidays. It went without saying she'd help any parent who required eleventh-hour child care.

As the demanding days rolled on, Cora gave a grateful sigh when Saturday arrived. Nap hours and feeding routines, arts and crafts, plus the preparation for the children's holiday singalong at the reception meant long hours. Much as she didn't want to admit it, sometimes she wished the holidays were over.

Sure, she embraced the jubilant enthusiasm, the cheerfulness, the merry decorations adorning neighborhood homes. She valued every precious minute.

But still ...

"There's no rest for the exhausted," she mumbled at eleven a.m. on Saturday. She'd set aside the day to complete her serious Christmas shopping.

Earlier that morning, she'd been too preoccupied with her holiday list to fuss with her appearance. She'd washed her hair and let it fall naturally over her shoulders. From her closet, she selected dark-wash jeans, a black and red tartan blouse and brown leather boots. A pair of festive Santa Claus earrings completed her ensemble.

List in hand and purse on her arm, she hurried to the front door.

The telltale crunch of car tires on her gravel driveway checked her steps.

Assuming the visitor wasn't her brother, because he was working a double shift at the hospital, she drew back the living room curtains and peered out the window.

A classic navy-blue Mustang sat parked in her driveway.

She opened the front door just as Patrick strode up the walkway.

"Hi, Cora." Clad in black jeans, boots, and a blue polo shirt that enhanced the heavenly deep blue of his eyes, his attractiveness was unquestionably lethal. Over his shoulder, he'd thrown a brown wool jacket.

"Hello, Patrick." She touched her throat. That enticing scent again—pine. "How did you find me?"

"It was easy." He smiled. "Every person I asked knew where you lived."

"In Bloomingfield?"

"I found a place on the outskirts and am almost halfway to Evanville. In any event, your fame covers miles." He kept his smile. "I was frustrated because I had to wait so long to see you again."

"You obviously succeeded, so your frustration has ended." She returned his smile and ushered him inside.

"I'm hoping if I ask you out in person that you won't refuse, since I went through all this trouble to locate you."

"You just said it was easy."

"Did I?" He regarded her from head to toe and smiled approvingly, as if she were the most beautiful woman on the planet. "You look gorgeous."

She ran a self-conscious hand through her hair. "Flattery will do little to persuade me."

"What about sincerity?"

Memories of his politeness while she'd fixed his car flooded back, drowning out the surprise of his arrival.

"Sincerity? In that case, a different story entirely." She hung her purse on the doorknob of the hall closet. "A sincere person is a rare and much-needed commodity these days."

"I agree."

Patrick was kind and treated her with respect. He gave and didn't seem to expect anything in return.

"Sincerity breeds trust," he maintained. "Which is important when establishing a successful relationship."

"You mean between us?"

"Exactly."

"We have a relationship?"

"Hopefully. Successful and otherwise ..."

His unexpected allusion—or was it a compliment?—brought a rush of pleasure to the pit of her stomach.

"Are you working today?" His smile filled the tight confines of the entryway.

"No."

"Wonderful. Neither am I."

"Happy coincidence, I'm sure." She bobbed her head as if she didn't believe him for a minute. "Is that why you're here?"

He opened his mouth, and she thought he'd crack a joke. Instead, he confirmed with a quiet, "I heard you usually had weekends off."

"From whom?"

"Oliver."

"You could have phoned instead of driving all the way from Bloomingfield."

"I didn't have your phone number."

She lifted a skeptical brow. "I'm fairly certain the same people who gave you my address and told you I took the weekends off would have also given you my number."

"Except talking to you in person is infinitely better."

Uncertain if she should agree or disagree, she merely shook her head.

In the limited time they'd spent together, Cora was certain of two things.

First, Patrick was a pro at small talk and compliments. And second, his male charm and persuasive smile were luring her ever closer to him.

Decisively, she took a step backward. She wasn't good at

any of this, and she certainly couldn't handle being so near him.

"Therefore, may I take you to lunch?" he asked.

"Therefore?"

He chuckled and gauged the distance between them before gazing down the hallway. "I'm guessing it isn't necessary to clean your refrigerator again."

"My refrigerator is spic and span."

He threw a teasing smile. "Mine could use a cleaning."

"Not on your life. Good try, though."

He laughed. "So, may I buy you lunch?"

"I admire your kindness and your unshakable effort—"

"Here comes the *but*," he murmured.

"*But* I've earmarked today for all my last-minute holiday shopping."

"Another happy coincidence. I wanted to finish today too, and we can shop together. After lunch."

She was about to speak, but he forestalled her.

"My dinner proposal was shot down twice," he reminded. "Now I'm determined to buy you lunch. If you refuse, I'll extend a breakfast invitation."

"Quite the strategy." She held off a grin. "Though it's kind of late for breakfast."

"Conversely ..." He peered at his watch. "It's not too late for lunch or dinner."

She vacillated.

"Let's go to that diner ... Olive's?" he suggested. "Allow me to repay you for fixing my car."

"How's the car acting?"

"Like a charm with its new battery. Although, the engine backfires."

"You might have too much fuel running to the cylinders."

"I had that checked. Regardless, if my car breaks down, I'm traveling with an expert mechanic."

Should she refuse again? A rebuff would be rude, and if this was a quick luncheon date, then the setting would be lively and open and hardly intimate. Totally relaxing in a cheery diner, savoring a deli sandwich and a cup of Oliver's delicious coffee.

Nevertheless, she was wary. Her attraction to him had swiftly reappeared, a reminder that Patrick was dangerously appealing.

Lost in thought, she repeated the vow she'd made to herself. After the shattering episode with Gregory, she never wanted to feel that precarious emotion called love again. Love was too painful, and she didn't trust her rash heart, nor her imprudent instincts.

Furthermore, the children in her day care were her main concern. If she allowed it, Patrick could become an all-consuming factor, and she wasn't prepared for a drastic change in her routine, especially one prompted by a compelling stranger.

But ...

Another but?

Sure, because he wasn't a stranger. He was a friend.

"My lunches consist of a hurried peanut butter and jelly sandwich." She pitched an additional excuse, anticipating it was enough for him to admit defeat.

"Fortunately, Oliver serves an extensive menu." Patrick smiled and motioned toward the door. "Shall we?"

"Perhaps in January," she hedged, realizing she was quickly running out of excuses. "I'm super busy, and my days are filled with a thousand extra tasks. You know how it is."

"Lunch isn't a task, Cora," Patrick replied as if he hadn't heard her. "Lunch is a necessity."

"I'm finishing my shopping today, remember?"

"Me too. Besides, I'd love to learn more about this quaint area I now call home. And ... I realize you like old cars." He studied her and paused. "The weather is clear so we can drive with the convertible top down. We might get chilly, but the car has an excellent heater."

She hung back on her heels and peered outside. "The weather *is* perfect," she said softly.

"Well?"

His lopsided grin brought a chortle to her lips.

How she loved riding in convertibles. She imagined the rush of wind on her cheeks, the crystal-blue sky, the silvery sun warming her face.

Besides, she liked lunch, she liked Oliver's Diner, and she liked Patrick.

Who could refuse?

She grabbed her purse, drew her red parka from the closet, and they headed out the door.

CHAPTER FOUR

*P*atrick knew the offer of a ride in his Mustang had steered Cora's decision in his favor. He'd rightfully anticipated she wouldn't refuse, and she hadn't. With that, the negotiation had been sealed, and expectation pulsed through him as he started the car. He was spending the afternoon with the enchanting, entrancing Cora.

She pulled down the visor, nudged aside her hair, and rummaged for an ivory comb in her purse. She tamed a stubborn curl by clipping it back and allowed her luxurious waves to spill over her shoulders.

"You're more stunning than a woman on the cover of a glossy magazine," he said.

"Glossy magazine?"

"Or any magazine."

"Thank you. You're very sweet." She pressed a forefinger to her grinning lips, then flipped the visor back into place.

Her face was clean and glowing, and his heart turned over at her wholesome beauty.

"The red color of the blouse complements your deep eyes," he cited.

"My eyes are deep?"

"Amber is striking and mysterious."

Before she replied, he inserted, "And your Santa earrings bring the finishing touch to a festive look."

His compliment was frank and judging by her smile, delighted her.

"So Santa earrings bring out the color of my eyes?" she challenged. "More than the reindeer earrings I wore the other day?"

He smirked. "Definitely a toss-up.

A short while later, the enticing whiffs of freshly baked bread and slow cooked meat welcomed them as they entered Olive's Diner. Patrick slid his arm casually around Cora as a waitress ushered them to a booth by the window, then promptly returned with two glasses of water.

He flicked a glance at the oversized booths covered in green plastic, the pink lights shining overhead, the fake potted poinsettia plants atop each table. In the corner, a skinny artificial fir tree glittered with silvery bulbs and a sprinkling of tinsel. Festive with a pinch of old-fashioned flair, the diner could have been featured on any iconic movie set depicting a vibrant Christmas scene.

A well-dressed older woman and a man in work clothes sat at the counter and they enthusiastically waved at Cora.

With a cheerful "Hello, how is your cottage by the sea?" Cora returned the wave.

"Fabulous!" they chimed in unison.

Patrick smiled an acknowledgement toward them. "Who are they?" he inquired.

"Emily Varon, or rather, Emily Vertucci and her husband, Joe. Emily frequented Olive's for dinner when she lived in Evanville. She and Joe met here, though now they're married and live in Cambria. Joe delivers chocolate to several shops, including Sally's."

"Sally, as in Oliver's girlfriend?"

"Yes. She co-owns Bloomingfield Candy Shop along with her brother, Ben." Cora indicated the parking lot. "There's Joe's truck, Moonglow Chocolatiers."

Patrick angled toward them. "They're an older couple."

"Both over the age of seventy, which proves love can happen at any age."

"They seem happy," he confirmed.

"Blissfully, judging from Oliver's sometimes long-winded commentaries."

So married people could be happy?

Patrick sat back and folded his arms, recalling the way his coworker Lorenzo beamed about his wife, Julie, but those expectations were shadowed by the memories of Patrick's demanding ex-wife, Olympia. Constant turmoil was the name of her game, and when they'd been married, he'd felt manipulated and constantly off-balance. His suggestions to seek guidance for their marriage had gone unheard.

"I love Christmas music," Cora was saying—no, singing about a button nose and corncob pipe. He grinned. His equilibrium was restored as he listened to her bright voice. "Can you think of a more favorable song for the holidays then 'Frosty the Snowman'?" she asked.

Actually, he could.

All I Want for Christmas Is You came to mind.

Now, why that particular song and that particular title? He kept the question to himself.

He wasn't a stranger to dating beautiful women, except this woman was fascinating, her heartwarming laugh irresistible. He drew a prolonged breath and allowed himself a thorough study of her face—a gorgeous brunette with the delicate features of a cherub.

"I don't hear any music except for your sweet voice," he noted.

"You will. Willie Nelson sings the greatest songs." She headed for the jukebox and dropped coins into the slot. Soon, a gravelly male began singing about a snowman called Frosty.

With her hands clasped behind her back and glossy hair framing her captivating face, Cora made her way back to the booth. She looked more like a college freshman than a woman in her thirties. (Patrick had inquired about her age too.)

As he admired her slow easy strides, he was catapulted back to a decade earlier, when, on his climb to the top of the proverbial news ladder, he'd married Olympia. He expected his high-society wife, the country club they joined, the brick mansion with, yep, a white picket fence, were all part of the happily-ever-after he envisioned.

It wasn't. He'd been wrong.

He recalled an adage his grandfather had recited on numerous occasions: "Youth is wasted on the young."

Wise words indeed.

Five years had passed, and Olympia was now a long-gone ex. In the interim, Patrick's imaginings of a carefree family crowded with giggling youngsters had been etched out.

He'd wanted children. Olympia had not. Why hadn't they discussed their priorities before marriage?

"Do you like the song I chose?" Cora slid onto the booth seat across from him.

He shifted his gaze to the jukebox. "Who doesn't wait all year for Willie Nelson to sing carols?"

"Ho, ho, ho." Cora sipped some water from her glass and gazed at him over the rim. "What's your favorite carol?"

"Hmm." He tapped his fingers on his bearded chin. "Difficult to choose."

"Surely one carol rises above the rest. A melody you never tire of."

He didn't particularly like Christmas carols and rarely sang, except in the shower where no one heard him. At the age of thirty-eight, he was jaded. Christmas had lost its spirit —somewhat because of the commercialism and never-ending media pressure to buy, buy, buy.

He expressed his observances aloud, and Cora quickly concurred.

"One benefit is that this season encourages people to help others," he said.

"Yes. Christmas is truly magical," she replied. "Or, rather, it used to be."

He settled his hands behind his head. "Why do you say that?"

"Lately, the season is a juggling act to accomplish more than I can ever get done."

"True," he agreed.

She pursed her lips. Nodded.

He drank more water.

"For countless families, the religious sentiment is forgotten." She clutched her fingers together. "Many children believe Christmas is mainly about presents. Too much money can be a bad thing."

"I like the giving gifts part." Patrick gazed down at his glass. "However, Christmas isn't really my thing."

Despite his response, she replied, "Even Mr. Scrooge came around in the end."

"Bah, humbug." Patrick flashed his most amiable grin. "Perhaps there's a chance for me after all."

"Most definitely."

Her words created an unexpected sense of optimism that flowed through his veins like a soothing balm.

"Choosing a unique present for someone you love is the best feeling, especially if you know it will bring them joy."

"A thoughtful sentiment behind the gift makes it even more special," he granted.

He left it at that. She acknowledged his statement with an adamant nod.

When he was married, he'd kept a running list on his computer of items Olympia wanted—mostly designer purses and shoes and costly perfume. Conversely, when it was a gift-giving occasion, she accepted his offerings with tightened lips. Soon afterwards, he'd learned why. She'd been having an affair with their next-door neighbor, a man twice her age.

His chest tightened. Their marriage had been built on lies and pretenses, and motherhood hadn't been part of the package.

"The children's parents and I want to observe the true Christian significance of Christmas," Cora was saying.

He drank some water. "I haven't been inside a church in years."

"I'm a churchgoer."

"Not me."

"Oh," she answered softly.

Oh?

A trace of sadness coupled with resignation crept into that one word, giving him the distinct impression that attending church was important to her.

"At any rate," he adeptly shifted the topic, "I prefer classical hymns. They're sung in church, correct?"

"All the time. Any hymn in particular?"

"Handel's *Messiah*." He suggested the first piece that came to mind.

"Hmm. Not exactly a hymn, but certainly inspirational. I'd categorize the *Messiah* as a large orchestral work."

"True." He preferred to watch hockey games or football over a concert. Nonetheless, he'd *heard* of Handel's *Messiah*.

Surely that counted, although he couldn't pinpoint how large a *large orchestral work* actually was.

Fortunately, she nodded as if she was completely satisfied by his claim.

Then she added, "Handel originally intended the composition for Easter week, not Christmas."

"Really?"

"Yes. He feared a London audience might not accept the piece because it was unorthodox, so he moved the premiere to Dublin, Ireland. He'd determined that the Irish audience was more sophisticated and elite than London."

"I never knew that. I'm spellbound."

"Are you now?" She laughed, and he laughed with her. He liked the sound of them laughing together.

"I love music," she reminded. "The *Messiah* is a true masterpiece."

"And you know a lot about it." *Apparently, much more than he did.* "On the other hand, I love facts, and I'll share these facts about the *Messiah* with Lorenzo. He's been singing Christmas melodies every day since I arrived at the studio."

"I'm aware." She laughed. "On the air, and both before and after your news reports."

"That's my job."

"You're an expert." She smiled, earnest and tender.

And there it was again. The tug on his heart.

He was hopelessly drawn to her sunny disposition, her never-ending enthusiasm, her appreciation for all things uplifting.

*O*nce they had ordered the luncheon special—a covered turkey sandwich drenched in brown gravy with a side of cranberry sauce—from their feisty middle-aged waitress who somehow pulled off calling Patrick "darlin'" and Cora "honey pie" without offending them; Patrick let the atmosphere of chrome and Formica countertops, and a rehash of Willie Nelson singing "Pretty Paper," to wash over him.

"So, you two are together once again." Oliver came to their booth wearing a red and white velvet Santa Claus hat. Across the front was embroidered the name *Sally*.

"Isn't your name, Oliver?" Patrick jested.

"Last I knew." Oliver bequeathed an all-encompassing smile as if he were truly Santa Claus catering to his customers. "But we all agree that Sally is prettier."

"The name or the person?" Cora teased.

"Both." Displaying his customary coffee pot, Oliver filled their cups, then placed sugar packets and a creamer on the table. He chatted with a combination of kindness and affable teasing. "I assumed Patrick intended to knock on every door from Bloomingfield to Evanville until he found you, Cora."

Patrick shifted and drew a bracing sip of hot black coffee. So absorbed in looking at her, he'd forgotten to load up his cup with cream and sugar.

"Enjoy lunch, you two." With a playful salute, Oliver marched to another table.

Cora lifted a dainty eyebrow. "What's this about knocking on every door?"

Patrick swallowed an unfamiliar constriction in his throat. "You want honest?"

"Absolutely. I believe in truth and honesty, remember?"

"I wanted to see you. How's that for honest?" He touched her palm. "Obviously, I'm not a pro on the best way to go about it. I didn't intend—"

"To declare it on local television?"

"Something like that." He fiddled with the plastic salt and

pepper shakers, a vintage pair of reindeers with bright-green bows.

"I'm flattered, Patrick," Cora said quietly.

He looked up at her. "You are?"

A rosy blush tinted her high cheekbones. "More than flattered."

He took several seconds to appreciate the lovely vision she created. The vivid tartan blouse enhanced her creamy complexion. Her lips, a rosy pink from the hot coffee, tempted him almost beyond reason. He could think of little else except kissing her.

Right there. In the diner. With Willie Nelson's raspy rendition of a Christmas carol in the background. He didn't regard Willie Nelson's music as romantic, but Cora probably did.

Patrick peered around, then gazed upward. Where was a mistletoe when you needed one?

Knowing Oliver, he would undoubtedly appear out of nowhere with a camera and begin snapping pictures if Patrick and Cora kissed. Or Emily and Joe would enthusiastically wave again.

While Cora scanned the dessert menu, Patrick scanned the other tables.

When he and Cora had first entered the diner, he'd wondered if all the customers had purposefully put down their forks, spoons and cups to regard them, because the diner had become so quiet.

He'd been wrong.

Now he *knew* they'd been staring because when he made eye contact, people grinned. Some entertained rambunctious children. Others were couples—both young and old. In any event he felt like E.T., an extraterrestrial oddity who had landed on earth after living on the moon. Or wherever E.T. lived.

Olive's Diner definitely was, as Cora described, "a place where all the patrons made it a point to know everyone else's business."

With a glib smile, he trained his gaze on the open case chock full of seasonal confections—mini cheesecakes, a classic red chiffon pound cake, and a triple layer chocolate torte iced with peppermint.

Although no one directly intruded, many people uttered hellos when they passed, and a youthful mother informed him, in a thick German accent, how she preferred his newscasts over the national media newscasters.

"*Danke,*" Patrick responded.

"*Danke?*" Cora repeated when the woman had crossed to another booth.

"I spent my childhood with my parents and grew up overseas," he explained.

"Just you? No siblings?"

"Just me."

"Do you see your parents often?"

"Not often enough." He splashed a couple ounces of cream into his coffee and stirred. Hopefully, that would finally cool it. "They're currently vacationing in the Bahamas."

"So, you're fluent in German?"

"For the most part."

"Do you speak other languages?"

"French, Dutch and Italian."

"You've seen countless countries." She clasped her hands. "I've never ventured any farther than visiting my mother in Nevada."

I'll take you anywhere you want, either here or abroad.

The words had just come, and he pondered if saying them aloud was too bold. Their friendship was fragile and scarcely beginning to blossom.

In the midst of his musings, their plates arrived.

Cora prayed a simple grace, and Patrick kept his head down and quietly whispered words he hadn't uttered since he was a child.

"Bless us, oh Lord ..." she uttered.

Then they relished a savory lunch, punctuated by the clinking of forks, laughter spilling from the counter where Emily and Joe sat, and Willie Nelson serenading the entire dining room with an upbeat rendition of "Deck the Halls."

An hour later, after they had declined dessert and chatted over coffee, Patrick placed two twenty-dollar bills on the table to ensure their waitress received a generous tip.

He thanked Oliver for the outstanding meal and top-notch service and claimed Cora's hand, pleased when she didn't object. He hadn't held a woman's hand since his divorce, and it felt good. It felt right.

Certainly, he'd dated, but dinners had consisted of polite exchanges with a woman over a meal. Nothing that would compel him to hold the woman's hand as they left a restaurant.

"You're lacking a mistletoe," Patrick mouthed when he caught Oliver's gaze. He tipped his head upward.

Oliver's eyes sparkled. "Excellent idea."

As Patrick and Oliver shared a wink, Cora asked him, "What's an excellent idea?"

Patrick didn't attempt to disguise his smirk. "Mistletoe hanging at the entrance to the diner."

"For kissing?"

"Why not?" He elected to go on a mistletoe hunt immediately.

She rewarded him with a spellbinding grin. There was nothing about her, he decided, that wasn't perfect.

"Instead of asking everyone in town where you lived," he joked as he held open the door for her to exit, "I should have hightailed it directly to Olive's Diner."

She chuckled. "Which is equivalent to placing a notice in the *New York Times*."

A while later, they reached Bloomingfield. Patrick found an excellent parking spot in the town center, and, cooled by the afternoon air, he assisted Cora with donning her parka, then slipped on his jacket.

As they sauntered along, townspeople approached Patrick to discuss one particular news item or another. Others greeted him and Cora with a heartening smile and moved on.

He noted the way folks regarded him and Cora together, surmising they were a couple. He liked that. He hadn't expected to, but he did. A stroll with Cora resembled a free fall, bringing a wide-range of sensations—most notably his stomach bending into knots whenever she glanced at him.

She cared for children and clearly loved them when she described several funny, mindful moments. Her melodic voice reminded him of an angel, and she lived in an area of California that could have been lifted straight out of a storybook.

"Am I invisible?" Cora half-laughed as another group headed toward Patrick. "You've lived here a week and are already well known."

He swept an arm around her as if it were the most natural gesture in the world. "Local folks recognize me because of my broadcasts." Politely, he answered questions while he drew Cora closer.

An elderly woman scrutinized them. "You must be Cora," she finally said.

"I am," Cora replied.

"Finally, Patrick found you." The woman wiggled sparse gray eyebrows, straight as pencils. "He asked everyone within a twenty-mile radius about you."

"Only twenty miles?" Cora twisted to him, her grin teasing.

"I'd search a thousand miles for you," he declared.

"Uh-huh." Cora rolled her eyes.

"When a man discovers a treasure, he will move mountains to find her," he said.

"Ooh, Miss Cora, he's a romantic guy," the elderly woman answered with a winsome grin. "I'd hold on to this anchorman if I were you. He's a keeper."

"Is there nothing secret in these towns?" Patrick chuckled.

"Absolutely nothing," Cora and the woman responded in unison.

After the woman waddled away, Cora paused. "Hold on. Rewind. I'm a treasure? No one ever called me that before."

He couldn't gauge her mood, but determined by her wide grin that she was truly charmed.

"A precious, wonderful treasure," he affirmed, tucking her hand in his.

She didn't pull away. An encouraging start. He could get used to strolling about this Norman Rockwell town holding Cora's delicate hand. She was gorgeous and hardworking, and her smiles came effortlessly. She was the essence of every trait that attracted him to a woman.

Besides, her scent brought whiffs of cinnamon and spicy vanilla, pure and fragrant. Wholesome as a bright winter day, he decided, as his pulse kicked up a notch.

She fell into an easy step beside him, their boots tapping on the sidewalk. On every street corner there was a gala celebration. To the marvel of the crowd, live reindeer pranced in a fenced in area near the town center.

"Fun fact," Patrick commented as they passed. "Reindeer don't fly, but some have a red nose."

"Wow. Brilliant." Cora giggled. "And you know this because ...?"

"I'm a science nerd."

"You are?"

He brushed up against her with a friendly nudge. "Get to know me better and you'll find out even more."

Slightly, her lips parted. "Is that a fact?"

He lingered, caressing his fingers across her cheeks. "It's a promise."

Sleds were set beside the reindeer, along with stacks of colorfully wrapped presents. The squeal of clamoring children prompted Patrick to laugh out loud.

"Are you enjoying yourself?" Cora asked.

"Immensely." He faced her, grinning in satisfaction. "Thank you for agreeing to share this day with me."

"I couldn't resist the offer to ride in a Mustang convertible," she goaded.

"With me."

Her features sobered. "With you."

A rush of emotion went through him he couldn't explain. He smiled, nodded. He couldn't remember later on if he thanked her for bringing such euphoria to a December afternoon.

Her cheeks had reddened because of the brisk temperature, or perhaps because of his remarks. In any event, she looked like she could use someone's arm around her to warm her. Fortunately, he was up to the task.

Star-colored beams shone across shop windows, illuminated by a light machine in the square. A jaunty rendition of "Up On the Housetop" performed by a community flute choir, filled the streets with a high piping sound. A gigantic fir tree blazed with white lights and sparkled with glass snowmen ornaments. Trace scents of candy apples and caramel corn floated through the air.

Cora's grin went from one ear to the other. "You might grow to love this season if you live here long enough."

He blew out a lengthy breath. "I don't plan on moving anywhere else."

"I was referring to Christmas."

"Christmas? That'll take some work."

He couldn't promise anything more, even to this perky woman with the sassy smile who was slowly invading his heart. That last Christmas with his ex-wife had commenced in endless arguments, completed by a separation. A man's heart could only take so much.

"There are heaps of upcoming kid-friendly events, including a coloring contest," Cora said.

"Do you take any of your day-care children to Bloomingfield?"

"I mostly stay in Evanville."

"And Evanville offers the 5K race," he said. "You're participating, correct?"

"Yes, I've decided to, and afterward a singalong with Santa is scheduled."

He snuggled her closer. "Will Willie Nelson make an appearance?"

"I seriously doubt it. And you can only participate in the singalong if you run the 5K."

"Why is that?"

"I don't know." She shrugged. "Rules are rules."

He smiled at her solemn declaration. A rule-follower. He liked that too.

She lifted a perfectly arched brow. "I meant to ask you ... you didn't sing with me when I sang in the diner."

"I sing ... sometimes, but not often. Besides, instead of popular carols I prefer ..." He faltered, trying to think of a high-brow piece of music. Brightening, he suggested Handel's *Messiah* again.

"You won't sing Willie Nelson but you'll sing the Hallelujah Chorus?"

"Certainly, at least in the shower." He tried to remember if he'd ever actually heard the 'Hallelujah Chorus.' He must have. It was a very famous piece.

"You sing all four parts?" Cora inquired. "Soprano, alto, tenor and—"

"Soprano ... usually."

"My word. You must have a high voice."

Evidently, he had gotten the sopranos mixed up with the tenors. Or was it the bass?

"I don't listen to a lot of holiday music," he replied, then changed the topic, hoping it would get him off the hook. "A certain someone suggested I remind them of Scrooge."

"Who?"

"You."

She granted another smile that caused his heart to beat double-time. They wended around a crowd of shoppers and Cora soon vanished into a candle store.

He waited outside. It allowed him to reflect on their day together.

Gradually, he was being led toward a beacon of hope— freshness and humor and goodness all rolled up into one beautiful woman. Whatever his former aspirations were in Raleigh, this was the day to realign them.

Cora reappeared, and they headed toward Bloomingfield Candy Shop.

The front window touted whimsical candy gifts molded into diverse shapes; and the signature chocolate-coffee fudge was arranged in bento boxes on a gold display shelf.

When they entered, the scent immediately transported Patrick back to his childhood. He drew in the heavenly sweetness and sugary bitterness, a chocolate-lover's dream.

Cora led him down the main aisle and introduced him to

Sally, the owner who stood behind the counter. Strains of "We Wish You a Merry Christmas" played as a backdrop.

Sally's response was a jubilant "Hello. Wonderful to meet you, Patrick."

She wore a red velvet suit, and a red and white Santa hat. Instead of *Sally*, the name *Oliver* was embroidered on the hat.

"You're the famous chocolatier," Patrick said.

Sally crinkled her eyebrows. "And you're the famous new anchorman on the six o'clock news."

He grinned. "I saw a hat just like yours when Cora and I lunched at Olive's today."

"I wish I could visit the diner more often, but the holiday season is very busy for both of us."

Patrick couldn't tear his gaze away from her hat. "Did you and Oliver switch hats?"

Sally pushed a strand of springy blond hair from her forehead. "It's a secret joke between us."

"Not that secret. Your names are emblazoned on each other's hats."

She leaned forward. Her blue eyes were remarkably observing as her gaze alternated between Patrick and Cora. "You are a stunning couple. Has anyone told you that yet?"

"Not till now," he replied. He was beginning to like Sally more and more.

"We're not a couple," Cora swiftly countered.

"But we could be," Patrick said.

"But we aren't."

"I agree with Patrick," Sally broke in.

"Praise you, Sally." Energized by her compliment, he decided this was the ideal opportunity to kiss Cora. He tugged her closer and brushed his lips across hers.

Sally applauded.

Cora did not.

"What was that for?" she demanded as she stepped back.

"The moment called for it."

"The moment? We're in the middle of a candy shop, which is hardly romantic."

Their gazes locked. He read the emotions in her eyes—apprehension, embarrassment, and something else. Attraction? He sincerely hoped so.

"No one is here except for the three of us." He tried a smile. "Next time I'll ask permission before I kiss you."

"Okay." Cora returned the smile, although it seemed a bit forced.

"This kissing chat is lovely, and I happen to think my shop is extremely romantic." Sally's gaze relaxed as she continued to gaze at them. "Besides, Patrick couldn't help himself. He was swept away by the ..."

"Chocolate," Cora put in.

"Charming woman beside me," Patrick affirmed.

He eyed Cora, who shook her head repeatedly.

"So," Sally motioned to the display case overflowing with sweets, "what can I help you with today?"

"I'm here to finish my holiday shopping," Cora said.

"Me too." Patrick gestured toward the doorway. "Sally, have you considered investing in a mistletoe? I suggested the same to Oliver when we were leaving his diner."

Cora rotated to face him. "If it were up to you, there would be mistletoe hanging all over town." She repressed a laugh which made Patrick breathed easier. Apparently he was forgiven for the spontaneous kiss.

Cora glanced at Sally and muttered, "He's impossible."

"Impossible men are the best kind," Sally said sagely.

"Are they?" Cora asked.

The opening of the shop's door interrupted the conversation.

Sally greeted the latest customer with a chirpy "Hello.

Please browse and let me know if there's anything you'd like to purchase."

The woman bobbed her head. "Thank you. I will."

As Cora began her candy selection, Patrick leaned against the counter, content to admire her lovely profile and a glimpse of her tantalizing lips.

"Where's your brother, Ben?" Cora asked Sally.

"He took the week off to travel to Alaska with Maise," Sally replied. "They're visiting her family."

"Maise is the local food critic," Cora explained to Patrick. "She and Ben are newlyweds."

Patrick tapped a finger on his bottom lip. "Are they happy?"

"Blissfully."

With a high chin, he whistled along with the holiday background tune. He was surrounded by happy couples. Maybe he and Cora would soon join the ranks.

Perhaps it was the drinking water in this part of California, he contemplated jokingly, although he knew it was something more, something better—honest, hard-working folks raising their families and truly caring for each other.

"Ooh, what kind of sweets are these?" Cora pointed to dozens of cookies displayed in the center of the case.

"Church window cookies. See? They resemble stained glass. Tara, my newest employee, baked them," Sally said. "They're quite popular."

Cora peered at the festive cookies dusted with coconut. "I'll take a dozen."

"Are they a gift?" Sally opened a white box and began arranging the cookies in a neat row.

"Yes. For myself." Cora laughed. "I'll freeze them. It's convenient to have extra cookies at the ready, especially when my brother returns from Nevada."

"Don't forget me," Patrick reminded.

"Never." She returned her attention to the display and Sally. "Jack likes peanut butter squares and I'll buy a box of caramels for my mother."

"What about your father?" Sally inquired rather loudly.

"He prefers dark chocolate." Cora's jaw clenched. She shrugged as if nothing was amiss, though something clearly was. "I'll purchase a pound. Regardless, it's not likely I'll see him."

"Where does he live?" Patrick asked.

"In Evanville."

"That's close. You'll probably see him."

"I probably won't." Her shoulders curled. "We had a disagreement."

Patrick searched her features. Clearly, she was upset. "Concerning what?"

She acknowledged his question with an airy wave. "Long story."

"Shall I ship the caramels to your mother?" Sally adeptly shifted the theme, before offering both Cora and Patrick a salted caramel sample. She then expounded on her recipe created with bittersweet chocolate.

"Infusion?" Patrick repeated. "Which means ..."

"I have no idea." Sally grabbed a candy for herself. "Actually, I do. It's—"

"Remarkable. I've eaten them before." Cora popped the candy into her mouth.

Patrick did the same. The explosion of creamy roasted cocoa on his tongue led to one word. *Amazing*.

Bloomingfield was definitely growing on him.

"Jack will hand deliver my mother's gift to her," Cora said. "He's flying a plane to Nevada."

"Your brother owns a plane?"

"His instructor is allowing him to fly hers, and she'll accompany him. From what I've gathered, she might be a love interest, but it's too early to tell. Up till now, he's been a confirmed bachelor."

"There's no better time for romance than the holidays." Patrick stepped aside as the other customer sauntered over balancing a jeweled gift tower filled with wrapped candy. She set it on the counter, then started for the coffee fudge with the promise that her order wasn't finished.

"My parents owned a plane." Patrick said quietly.

Sally sucked in a short breath. "They did?"

"Yes, they were both diplomats."

"I'm definitely in the wrong profession." Sally groaned and leaned over the counter.

Cora froze in place and studied him.

He reached out to grab her hand.

She shook him off. "Wealthy diplomats?" Her gaze narrowed.

"My parents are well off. They own a home in the Bahamas."

Cora swallowed. "You told me they were vacationing there."

"They are. In their second home."

He recalled her comments about too much money being a bad thing. Nonetheless, he'd made it on his own and never sought financial help from his parents. They'd worked full time for years and deserved to reap the benefits of their hard-earned retirement in style.

"Patrick, I heard you dined at my sister's restaurant last night with Lorenzo." Sally stepped in.

"The Pasta Junction." He patted his stomach, answering Sally as Cora continued to watch him. "Lorenzo insisted I taste Julie's fettuccini, and I was more than happy to accommodate, although by the time we arrived the dinner hour was long over."

"That didn't stop you, though," Sally teased.

"I never refuse homemade pasta leftovers."

Sally's attention wavered between Patrick and Cora. She paused. "Why don't you both come to the Christmas Eve buffet?"

"I can't," Cora uttered quickly as Patrick replied, "Sounds marvelous."

He wished to see her, and his wish magnified as he gazed at her exquisite face. "Why not?" he urged. "The food is first class."

"I attend church service."

"So do we," Sally chimed in. "We'll dine together afterward. My daughter will be with me, of course, and Oliver will accompany us after he closes the diner."

"Sounds like an excellent plan, Cora," Patrick said. "After my broadcast, I'll drive to Evanville to pick you up. We can meet everyone there."

He smiled. Everything was being arranged perfectly. Except for convincing Cora.

"I can't," she said.

Sally boxed up the cookies and handed the package to Cora, her smile laced with irritation. "You won't be watching any children, correct?"

"On Christmas, all the kids will be with their parents."

"We've solved your church service conflict and you aren't working. Therefore ..." Patrick said optimistically.

"Sorry."

"Christmas Eve is special and I will not allow you to spend another Christmas alone." Hands on her hips and totally in her element behind the cash register, Sally looked completely self-assured. "That's an order from a dear friend."

Cora opened her mouth, then closed it.

"Super and settled. We'll have a festive and fun holiday." Sally spun to Patrick. "My store ships everywhere, by the way. May I suggest some boxes of coffee fudge with your order?"

"Your infusion candy is utter perfection. Make it two boxes."

"Of infusion candy?"

"Absolutely."

"And the fudge?"

"Sure."

Cora sent him a surprised look. "You're purchasing a lot of candy. I hope there are dentists open in the Bahamas during the holidays."

"There are. My parents love anything sweet and I obviously take after them." His gaze moved tellingly to her lips.

"Excellent." Sally's sweeping flourish got his attention. "Three boxes of infusion candy and two boxes of coffee fudge shipped to the Bahamas."

He nodded his assent.

Sally rang up his order and greeted the sum with a smile. "Ninety-five dollars."

He studied the receipt. "Does the total include the shipping charge?"

"Nope. In addition, I'll pack an extra dozen cookies— your choice—a treat your parents can indulge in."

"At no charge?"

"I'm a businesswoman. There's always a charge."

"Fine. Thanks."

His gaze found Cora's.

"You should be concentrating on your candy purchases, not me," she admonished.

"I have a unique talent. I can focus on numerous topics at once."

Sally rang up a new total and presented it to him with an effervescent smile.

He leaned forward and gasped.

"Are you certain about your focusing skills?" Cora goaded while Sally explained that shipping was expensive because chocolate required cushioning, packaging and refrigeration with cold packs.

Clearly outmaneuvered, he bobbed his head.

Sally was hands down the finest salesperson in the entire state of California.

What's more, maybe his concentration wasn't as good as he assumed, at least not when the lovely Cora was anywhere in the vicinity.

CHAPTER FIVE

On the return drive to Evanville, Patrick debated whether to broach the subject of the Christmas Eve buffet with Cora, and decided to wait a few days. Surely with Sally and her family in his corner, she wouldn't refuse.

Once they were on the road, Cora settled into the passenger seat and stretched out her legs "Tell me more about yourself," she encouraged.

He described his newscasts in detail, minutely examining and evaluating his on-air segments.

"I want to gain a better understanding of you—the person," she stated when he finished.

He preferred learning more about her, but quickly explained that he'd decided to major in journalism as soon as he'd completed high school. After graduating from an Ivy League university with a master's degree, he spent the next ten years traveling around the world as a major news correspondent.

She sat straighter. "What countries?"

"The UK, Asia and Australia, mostly. Or, wherever there was a story." He'd accumulated a staggering amount of money in the process and had bequeathed a substantial amount to various charities—most notably an organization that raised money for safe playgrounds that were also handicap accessible.

Casually, her hand touched his. "And then?"

"I was offered a studio position with a 24/7 cable news network." He slanted her a smile. "I applaud your interest, although all this talk centered around me is quite enough."

"I like learning about you."

He gave a crisp nod. "Why?"

"Because I like ...*you*."

Her straightforward response made his heart pitch.

There was an attraction between them she obviously couldn't deny. Neither could he.

She glanced away when she recognized his appreciative gaze and studiously inspected her hands. "Sounds like you were rising the ladder of success."

"I certainly tried." He grinned in spite of himself. She'd summed up several years of his life accurately. "Nonetheless, I have complete confidence that the new anchorman in Raleigh who succeeded me is amassing an avid following."

"If you're correct," she noted with an infectious smile, "I assume his communication and improvisation skills are outstanding and he can think on his feet. Plus, he projects a professional image because you're the best newsman on television. I wouldn't want to be in his shoes and tread on the heels of your footsteps."

"Thank you, although you may be biased."

"For what reason?"

"Because we're on our first date, and I assume you wouldn't say anything negative about me."

"We're on a date?" Her eyebrows furrowed. "We had lunch and then Christmas shopped."

"We're enjoying our time together and therefore, this is a

successful date. Consequently, your opinion of my broadcasts are probably biased."

"True," she confirmed with an indulgent laugh.

He found her honesty welcoming and felt that familiar tilt of his heart.

"Thus, accepting this anchor position in Bloomingfield is a step up?" He heard the unexpected sensitivity in her tone and caught a glimpse of her puzzled expression.

"In truth, the position is exactly the opposite." He kept his hands on the steering wheel. Traffic was light and easy—another positive aspect of small-town living.

"I'm surprised," she said. "You seem like a go-getter."

"I am. I was." He considered how best to reply and chose forthrightness. "I prefer to report on the little things that touch the lives of people I knew, rather than massive world affairs that are overwhelming at times and seemingly impossible to cope with."

She studied him for a beat. "You willingly gave up an exciting career."

"I'm in a different season now." Not to mention that Cora fit into the new life he longed to find. She was energetic, attractive, and appreciative of what was right in front of her —not searching for an unattainable rainbow.

Wasn't joy found in the minute, everyday occurrences?

He needed to feel grounded again, calm again. He needed to breathe without the overwhelming strain of a fast-track lifestyle.

He darted a glance at her and imagined kissing her.

His hand grasped hers, and she smiled. He reciprocated, feeling a bit rash for his adolescent pleasure in the simple touch of her fingers.

Certainly, he wasn't falling in love. After a sorry marriage to a woman more interested in his connections and affluent lifestyle than in him, he was skeptical of anything remotely resembling love.

Cora switched on the radio and discovered a station featuring holiday tunes. Within minutes, "A Holly Jolly Christmas" blared from his Mustang's eight speakers, and she hummed along. "This is one of the songs my day care children are singing for our annual program," she managed to tell him between lyrics.

He maneuvered around a parked car, then stopped at a traffic light at the next intersection. "How many songs are you preparing?"

"Three. 'A Holly Jolly Christmas,' 'It Came Upon A Midnight Clear,' and 'Silent Night.' We rehearse every day and will present a concert to the parents before holiday break."

"The kids are memorizing all those words?"

"We keep it simple, holly and jolly." Her buoyant rejoinder was muffled as she turned the volume louder and sang the second stanza in a tone that was definitely easy on the ear.

The hours ticked by in a blink.

They exited the highway onto the two-lane road to Evanville, and his car topped the hill to her bungalow with ease. The afternoon had bowed to early nightfall. Bold hues of orange and gold stretched across the sky and Cora's features glowed, her gaze drifting upward to the first stars in the sky.

As they entered her driveway, her eyes widened and she raised her voice with an emphatic no!

"What's wrong?"

"I have motion detector lights."

"Really?" He motioned to her darkened house. "Where?"

"They aren't working and I need *new* ones." She let out a peal of laughter.

"Am I missing something?" He turned off the car's ignition. "Is needing new lights somehow funny?"

"Not the lights. The word *new*." She wiped tears of hilarity that had gathered at the corner of her eyes. "And I must figure out my wish before it's too late."

"What wish?"

She shook her head and refused to elaborate.

Her comment merely heightened his fascination. He'd never met a woman like her—car mechanic, businesswoman, and a loving daughter and sister.

He insisted on opening the passenger door for her, hoisted her packages from the trunk and walked beside her. The evening breeze was crisp, and he breathed in a lungful of refreshing air.

When they reached her porch, she lingered.

"Would you like to come inside for coffee?" She rushed her words, louder than usual. Her fingers touched her throat in an absent form of a question. Already, he was associating these subtle little movements to her.

"For coffee?" he repeated.

On the one hand, yes. On the other hand, definitely yes.

A puff of wind teased her hair. Absently, she pushed it aside. "Or tea or a soft drink, if you prefer."

"Coffee is fine." He preferred to crack open a cold soda, but settled on the coffee. He would have eaten a live octopus to spend more time with her. Casually, he slid his hands into his pockets so he wouldn't appear too eager. "Oliver has certainly mastered the art of hot coffee."

"Coffee is my specialty too."

"Hot?"

"Piping," she assured.

Inside the foyer, she peeled off her parka, and he shrugged off his wool coat. She hung them both in the closet. While she placed her various Christmas gifts on closet shelves, he made amiable remarks about all the delicious candy she'd purchased, and she enthusiastically concurred.

They walked into her living room and she switched on a couple of side lamps, which cast a rosy glow into the room, and his appreciative gaze glided over her magnificent hair, and the glint of glossy russet highlights.

"You're staring at me," she said.

"I am?" He'd perfected his innocuous smile.

Her eyes twinkled. "Yes."

"I can't help it." He brushed a strand of hair from her temple.

He stepped back and scanned the room furnished with an overstuffed armchair, a rocker-recliner and a sofa, all covered in a tan plaid fabric and blanketed with knitted quilts. Warm and inviting without pretense, the room was ideal for holding a restless child or rocking a toddler to sleep.

Wall-mounted shelves held an assortment of toys, jigsaw puzzles, a pyramid of books and numerous teddy bears. Mittens and thick wool socks were folded beside a miniature pine tree arranged on a shelf.

"No holiday wreaths?" he asked. "You, the Christmas elf herself?"

"I'm mindful of tiny hands yanking down decorations and injuring themselves. I'll trim the outside of my house soon, but the inside can wait. Normally, I only put up a small tree, anyway." She gave a tiny laugh. "Will you decorate your place?"

"I'm still unpacking boxes in my apartment." He cocked his head. "Besides, Christmas isn't really my—"

"Your thing. Yes, so you've said. Please make yourself comfortable." She gestured to the sofa and disappeared into the kitchen.

Flanked by a pair of gray textured curtains, a sliver of moonlight shone through the window. Already understanding who she was—organized and disciplined—he wasn't surprised by the room's neatness. Those attributes, combined with understanding, altruism, and tenderness, were essential in running a successful day care.

He sank into the timeworn sofa, contemplating the great lengths Cora went through to clean her home every day after the children left.

His ex, on the other hand, had been the poster child for messiness, and he'd constantly tripped over her extravagant dresses and costly shoes strewn all over the floor. Certainly, her disregard for orderliness had underscored his overheavy work load.

Cora reappeared carrying a tray with two mugs of steaming brewed coffee, spoons, and napkins. She'd also included a glass creamer and sugar set. She drank her coffee black, but she'd obviously noticed his penchant for heaps of sugar and cream from their lunch in the diner.

He concealed his delight for her thoughtfulness with a heartfelt thank you.

She set down the tray and settled opposite him on the sofa.

"So, where were we?" she asked.

"About what?" He spooned three teaspoons of sugar into his mug, poured cream to the top and stirred.

"About you," she replied. "Your career move to Blooming-field is hardly your entire life."

"I gave you my narrative and there's nothing else to tell." He took a gulp of coffee. Fragrant, delicious ... and boiling hot. He blew on the coffee. It didn't help, and he scalded his tongue a second time.

"Everyone has more than one story."

He sat on the sofa's edge. "I haven't heard yours yet."

"As I mentioned, I've lived in Evanville my entire life and am thoroughly content." She raised her mug in a toast.

He heeded, and they clinked mugs.

"To contentment," she said.

"To contentment." He repeated. "Now tell me about yourself."

She wrapped her fingers around her mug. "I've always adored children, so opening my own business and tending to them is a dream come true." She inclined her head. "Now it's your turn."

"Again?"

"Absolutely."

"Okay. On one condition."

"Which is?"

"Sit closer."

He'd never shared his difficult years in grade school with anyone. In several he attended, he'd been teased for being overweight and frequently nicknamed Pudgy Patrick.

No, he decided. Not that story.

Perhaps he could muster up an amusing memory.

"Why?" she was asking.

"Why what?"

"Why sit closer?"

Involuntarily, he held his breath as a heartbeat went by. "Because I want to put my arm around you, and I can't if you're sitting on the other end of the sofa."

Warily, she swallowed coffee.

"You can trust me," he assured. "There's no mistletoe in sight. Which, in case you haven't noticed, seems to be the norm in this part of California."

A smothered half-laugh was his answer, resulting in her query, "How do I know for sure?"

"About a mistletoe? Look up."

She grinned. "How do I know about *you*?"

"I'll give you two reasons."

She waited. He liked the way her generous lips tilted up.

"First, you can always trust me. I'll ask your permission before I kiss you, and I never go back on my word."

She seemed to relax. "And the second reason?"

He leaned forward and lifted his mug. "I'm a man who holds hot coffee in high esteem."

"What?" She blinked. "You realize your explanation makes no sense."

He inflated his sigh. "You got me there."

Her shoulders shook with a choked laugh as she sat back.

His amber-eyed beauty. Every minute with her was a precious gift. And he craved more—endless hours—to ease into her approach to a slower-paced lifestyle.

In the ensuing hour, they discussed her childhood and her brother, Jack, who was a nurse at the hospital. A discussion came next regarding her parents' divorce.

Zoe, Cora's mother, lived in Nevada whereas Cora's father had always made his home in Evanville, much like Cora. Observing Cora's expression whenever she mentioned him, Patrick asked a question of his own.

"Are you and your father arguing about something?"

The upbeat mood of the previous hour vanished.

Briefly, she closed her eyes. "Why do you ask?"

He slipped an arm around her shoulders. "You're somber all of a sudden."

"We had a disagreement." Her cheeks reddened. She plucked a tiny loose thread from the sofa. "Actually, we've had numerous arguments—especially in the last few years."

Alerted to her studied nonchalance, Patrick tipped up her head. She blinked back the tears filling her eyes.

"What do you need?" he asked.

"I'm not sure."

"You're not alone. I'm here."

"I don't know where to begin."

"I care about you, Cora. I'll listen if you want to talk.""

Her features eased, though her chin lifted, as if defending herself. "Recently, he called me an unkind name and told me in no uncertain terms that I was desperate."

"Desperate about what?"

"Dating. Men." Her small hands fisted. "Since he and my mother divorced, his remarks have become snide and unsettling—especially about my being so thin. They hurt."

Inwardly, Patrick winced. "You're lovely."

Her fists relaxed. "Hardly ..."

Almost too stunned to speak, Patrick replied, "You're his precious daughter. Surely he argued in anger."

"His remarks still hurt."

"I'm sorry. Truly."

"Our most recent argument involved a guy I was dating." She rubbed her arms. "My father hated him."

"Why?" Patrick didn't expect the jealous pang in his chest at the image of Cora with another man. "Did this guy abuse you?"

"I never met him."

Patrick frowned. "You dated a guy you never met?"

"We corresponded through a dating website."

"Who is he?"

"No one important." She clasped her fingers together and avoided his gaze.

"Does he have a name?"

"Sure. Con man." Her laugh was strained. Her hands fell limp in her lap. "In retrospect, I should have known. The warning signs flashed loud and clear, and my father offered countless objections and cautionary advice."

"Which apparently you didn't heed."

"On top of that, he hired an investigator to prove to me that the guy wasn't real."

"Was he right?"

"Yes."

"Your father truly cares about you."

"It's just that he's always so hard on me, you know? My guard went up." She rolled her shoulders. A tiny scowl marred her features.

"Understandable."

With a slow, unsure head shake, she asked, "Have you ever read the story, *A Christmas Carol*?"

Taken aback, he gazed at her. "Uh, huh. Why?"

"The ghost of the future made Scrooge realize he only cared about himself."

"If you're referring to your father, then remember the end of the story. Scrooge changed and became the most beloved man in town."

"Meaning?"

"People change. People are forgiven, especially if they genuinely love you."

"Forgiveness is hard." She exhaled. "Any advice?"

"Wipe the slate clean and let go of your resentments."

She didn't move. Neither did Patrick.

Finally, he whispered, "May I?"

She lifted her head. A tear trickled down her cheek. They were so close he heard her pounding heart and his own thudded in response.

Gently, he brushed her tear away and kissed her forehead, before his lips moved smoothly over hers.

When she broke the kiss, he didn't press her further.

"So now you know my sad story," she said in a low voice.

"And I'm here for you."

He gazed at her perfect profile and righteous anger flooded through him. She had experienced betrayal, then embarrassment, all because a con man had taken unfair advantage of her. He could scarcely imagine Cora's disbelief when she discovered the truth.

He grazed his lips over her fragrant hair. "A word of advice from someone who doesn't know all the answers, or, in reality, any of them."

She grinned, and he took that as an encouraging sign to continue.

"Your relationship with your father is important. If you hold on to anger, it will build resentment and eventually harm you, not your offender."

She dipped her head. Sighed. "You could be a counselor, you know that? You're good to talk to."

"I'm happy being a small-town newscaster."

"Now it's time for you to tell me more about yourself."

"More? Again?"

"Totally."

He took a sip of coffee.

He wasn't sure how to begin. But he was here with Cora, and he knew he could tell her anything and she would be understanding.

Beneath the brilliance of her sweet smile, he fixed his gaze on his hands.

"I realized a hard lesson when I discovered my wife was cheating on me," he began.

His lawyer had used the word *cuckolded*. It had seemed ridiculous at the time, (who used that word?) but resonated 100 percent true.

"I'm sorry, Patrick."

"Don't be. It was eye opening, though our marriage hadn't been good for several years. I ignored the discontent because I was so bent on reporting."

"You didn't try to resolve your differences?"

"Of course. Then again, it takes two people. I wanted the

all-American dream life. She chose high society and incessant travel."

"Define it. The dream life."

Living a life with you, he thought as he gazed at her. Her sweetness was a gift to be embraced.

Aloud, he replied, "After my divorce, I assumed a happily-ever-after was elusive."

"And now?"

Quietly, he brushed his knuckles across her cheek. "Now I'm beginning to believe that true happiness is within reach."

Her face colored, and his heart curved toward her as it always did when she regarded him like that.

For a long moment she rested her head on his shoulder. Soothingly, he rubbed her back. She fit perfectly beside him, as if they had always been together.

The room was quiet. Church bells pealed in the distance. From her window, sparkling silver lights from the neighbors' houses twinkled.

Words weren't required, only the comfort of companionship.

Soon she fell asleep, and he wrapped his arms around her. He regarded her exquisite face in repose, and his fingers eased the dark hair from her temples.

Sometime later she awoke with a start, blinked up at him and rubbed her eyes. "Oh, Patrick, I'm sorry. I'm obviously not a good hostess."

"Don't apologize." He smiled at the disconcertment in her voice. "You slept a half hour at most."

"Still—" She shifted and his arms tightened protectively around her.

"You work too hard," he said.

"Not any harder than you." She slid from his grasp. "'Tis the season for busyness and obviously in my case, exhaustion."

"I thought it was the most wonderful time of the year."

She smiled. "Of course, but it's also crazy and stressful."

"I hope to simplify my life and focus on what really matters," he said. "That's the reason why I moved here."

"Here's a secret," she informed him with a sparkle in her deep-colored eyes. "Stay positive, no matter what."

"Like you?"

She nodded several times. "I try."

He basked in the enthusiasm of her gaze, then reluctantly checked his watch. "I overstayed my welcome. Sorry."

"No, not at all. Thanks for the company."

He stood when she did, and she walked with him to the entryway.

He wanted to see her again. That's all there was to it. But how? They both worked full-time Monday-through-Friday jobs, and he oftentimes worked extra hours depending on breaking news.

Still, where there was a will ...

"Cora," he started. "When can—"

Her cellphone chirped, and she excused herself to retrieve it. She glanced at the caller ID and paled.

"It's my father," she announced quietly.

"Take the call."

"I'm not prepared to talk." Her voice caught. "Should I?" Her gaze drifted to Patrick and then back to the phone.

He nodded. "Definitely."

As she clicked the phone on and launched into a discussion, Patrick retrieved his coat and opened the door to let himself out. He had hoped the evening would end with another kiss. The spontaneous kiss in the candy shop hardly counted, and the one on the sofa hadn't lasted nearly long enough.

He glimpsed her, standing at the window, her body rigid in conversation.

Could she mend the differences with her father?

Once more, he reflected on the book, *A Christmas Carol*. Well-loved and timeless, the tale was one of forgiveness and repairing broken bonds.

Peace and harmony. What better season than the holidays?

CHAPTER SIX

*H*ow long could a plain woman like her hold his interest?

Cora couldn't. She was average—someone who did everyday chores and led an everyday life.

Patrick's silver-spoon background had been enriched by foreign cultures. Furthermore, his job offered him entrée to the powerful, wealthy and distinguished. Hers gave her chattering kids playing catch in her enclosed backyard. Or tugging on her arm. Or whispering in her ear.

Consequently, as much as she'd enjoyed her shopping day with him, she was wary.

Wary because she found herself falling in love with him.

Her soulmate. Her partner. The right man.

It had happened quickly and without explanation. Now, her mind focused on him when she should be concentrating on other things—namely giving the children her unflagging attention, or the thousand chores begging to be accomplished.

She was confronted with chaotic days, her hours filled with a wailing twin who sounded like he'd been mortally wounded when he'd merely been egged on by his brother. Or, a pig-tailed girl screaming bloody murder when a freckled-faced boy chased her around the yard waving a grasshopper. Which, incidentally, turned out to be a leaf.

For the most part, though, the children were amazingly obedient. Nevertheless, by day's end, both Cora and Molly were tired.

As the week progressed, three youngsters had meltdowns from holiday overload; cookie baking to be finished with the older children; and a couple of parents dropped by unexpectedly, begging Cora to watch their child for an hour or two between Christmas and New Year's.

She never refused, though she worked out a schedule that was also fair for her. Per her exchange with Patrick, she'd decided the upcoming break was essential for her sanity and well-being.

Every night after the news aired on television, he would phone her.

The first night he inquired about her phone discussion with her father.

"We're taking it slow and easing back into our relationship," Cora summarized. "I've established boundaries beginning with no name calling or personal attacks."

"You're off to a good start," Patrick encouraged. "Remember, no parent is perfect, so strive for honesty."

"I am. We both are. I want stable, healthy communication and my father agrees."

"Stick with reaching a common ground and keep your expectations realistic."

Patrick was right, and she grinned. "You really should consider counseling in your spare time."

His chuckle was deep. "Thanks, but I'll pass."

The next evening, he cut their talk short because of a news story.

The following evening, he interrupted their phone conversation mid-way with, "Hang on, Cora." He murmured to someone in the background, then came back on the line.

"You're still at the station? It's nine o'clock at night." She kept her tone neutral, refusing to criticize him for working constant overtime.

"I arrive early and stay late. Tonight, I edited a story right up until I was on the air."

"The one about the local health-care industry?" she asked. "Your questions and ideas were spot-on."

"Thanks. Community commitment will generate a tremendous difference and—"

As she'd learned from earlier discussions, he reviewed his news hour almost as if it were a complicated sculpture to be painstakingly assessed. In fact, he was so critical of himself, she'd perfected the excuse of using the weather to change the subject.

"Hang on. Someone is insisting on an answer to a story question." Patrick muffled the receiver, returning a minute later. "Sorry. I gotta run. I'll call you tomorrow, okay? I'm looking forward to seeing you."

"Sure."

"Sure? You can do better than that. I think about you constantly."

And I think about you. But she didn't tell him that. Instead, she wished him a restful night and clicked off.

In the silence of her living room, Cora asked aloud, "Why don't our calls ever last longer than fifteen minutes?"

The answer rang as loud as a silver steel bell. Their spheres were simply too different.

When next he phoned, his voice was heavy. "Sometimes categorizing a new job as demanding is an understatement," he said.

Her heart twisted in frustration. "Bloomingfield isn't bringing the satisfactory life you imagined?"

"I'm to blame, not the town." He drew in a sharp breath. "I'm finding it hard to let things go and let anyone else do my job."

"Ah, you're unquestionably a perfectionist," she noted.

"The holidays, combined with a brand-new station and the move ..." She envisioned his handsome face, his eyebrows furrowed into a troubled frown. "Cora, I can't wait to see you, but I don't want to schedule a date I'll have to cancel."

*U*nfortunately, that was exactly what happened.

The next day, he asked her to dine with him at The Pasta Junction on Friday because he was only working the afternoon shift.

She agreed.

After she had taken extra care to wear a silver sequined top and black wool slacks, secured her freshly washed hair in place with a satin headband, and teetered in four-inch heels (that she knew she wouldn't be able to walk in for more than an hour), he apologetically phoned and explained in a direct, but awkward manner that he was forced to cancel. He'd been called on assignment to Bloomingfield's town center to conduct spontaneous, on-camera interviews with local shoppers and couldn't refuse.

Fearful her disappointment might show, she blithely told him she understood and not to fret, refusing to sound pathetic.

"I'm sorry," he murmured.

She nodded into the phone.

"I miss you."

She squeezed her eyes closed. "I miss you too."

Sensing his sense of urgency to go, she swallowed. "Good night, Patrick."

"Sweet dreams, beautiful."

When the call ended, she yanked off her heels and sank onto the floor. Restlessly, she fidgeted with the silver bracelets on her wrist.

She'd chosen an outfit other than jeans and a sweatshirt, partly to dress appropriately for the exclusive Italian restaurant, partly to impress him.

With a grim, short laugh, she slumped against the wall. Although she shook her head in denial, the realism was that she was beginning to care too much for him. And caring for a man led to regret, and a bruised heart.

The hard fact was that he'd chosen his work over their date, and, after ruminating over that for a while, her pride forced her chin up.

She straightened, flew into the kitchen and combed the freezer. Quickly, she polished off the entire box of church window cookies from Sally's chocolate shop, allowing a thaw for only a few seconds in the microwave first.

Yes, the eating was emotional, but the occasion called for a sugar rush. Her father had once suggested she was too skinny, anyway.

*B*ecause their Friday night date hadn't panned out, Patrick promised himself he would echo the previous Saturday and spontaneously show up at Cora's house. However, a breaking news report on a mudslide in the mountains occurred before dawn, and he headed to the on-site location.

The mudslide situation was resolved by midafternoon, and he got into his Mustang and drove straight to Evanville.

He still wore the tailored gray slacks, long-sleeved green polo, and a twill jacket, and didn't bother to change.

When he pulled into Cora's driveway, he found her stringing net lights around her outside bushes.

"Surprise!" He rushed forward and almost collided with her as she spun.

"Patrick ... hello." She smoothed her candy-cane-striped sweatshirt over worn jeans. A pair of silver star earrings dangled from her ears. "I didn't expect to see you this weekend."

"I should have called first, but last Saturday's plans worked out and I hoped this Saturday would as well. I'm sorry about canceling last night."

"I understand. I'm thrilled you're here." A smile flickered across her expressive face—no trace of anything but happiness. He imagined sealing that happiness with a kiss.

The connection between them was real, and he knew she sensed it too.

With an absolute strength of willpower, he stayed where he was and didn't sweep her into his arms. He'd just arrived and the entire afternoon stretched ahead of them. Besides, there was no mistletoe in sight.

"The lights look good." He motioned to the bushes, then to her. "And you look even better."

She looked better than better. She looked exquisite. He cleared his throat, aware of the husky romanticism in his voice.

"I haven't plugged the lights in yet," she reminded.

He ducked his head. "Oh, right."

Once, he'd believed himself a talented conversationalist. Apparently, he was wrong because he was comparing Cora to a set of darkened lights.

"I bought *new* lights and a *new* motion detector." She laughed, exactly as she had the week before.

He was about to inquire about the funniness of all things new when she plugged in the lights. They illuminated her house with a silvery-white glow, and she smiled with a radiance that brought his self-control to a standstill.

He stepped closer.

She regarded him with wide-eyed innocence. "Did you want to say something about the lights?"

"I wanted to say something about you." He brushed his lips on hers. "Thanks for being so forgiving and patient."

"You're welcome. Since you're here I'd offer dinner, though I'm not much of a cook."

"My specialty is frozen pizzas."

"Grocery shopping is my least favorite chore and my kitchen is essentially food-less," she said.

"I'll treat you to Olive's Diner, providing there's a Saturday special."

"You're extremely generous, Mr. Gervez." She swallowed a burst of laughter. "Allow me a few minutes to change, and I'll take you up on your offer."

*W*hen they arrived at the diner, they chose their customary booth by the window.

Several customers' eyebrows rose, particularly Oliver's. "You're becoming my new regulars, and I sense a romance blooming." He set down menus. "Our special this evening is a mistletoe offering—barbecued chicken, marinated mushrooms, your choice of two sides and a slice of red velvet cake."

"A mistletoe menu?" Patrick peered at the ceiling. "Where's the mistletoe?"

Oliver chuckled. "I concentrate on the food."

"Some things never change," Patrick muttered.

Stifling a laugh, Cora headed for the jukebox. The diner

was packed with people she obviously recognized, and she paused to chat with friends.

When she made her way back to their booth, a woman shouted their names.

Sally waved from behind the counter.

Oliver might not have gotten around to the mistletoe, but he'd placed a miniature white snowman clad in a green jacket and scarf beside the cash register. "I'm assisting Oliver," Sally declared, "because he's busy on Saturday evenings and my candy shop closes early."

"Is your daughter here?" Cora called out.

"Clarissa is in the kitchen helping a waitress sort red velvet cakes. I'll send her over for a quick hello."

Patrick turned to Cora. Her crisp white blouse, black jeans, and decorative wide red belt around her slim waist suited her. With tousled hair skimming her shoulders in velvety-smooth waves and festive star earrings, she emanated holiday perfection.

He stretched out his legs, relishing a pleasant evening. Christmas in a tiny community was special, especially when he shared it with Cora.

When their meal was finished, they spent a few minutes at the counter conversing with Oliver, Sally, and Sally's adorable daughter, Clarissa. Judging from the number of customers who came over to chat, Cora was a well-loved care-giver. Likewise, their admiration for her seemed to embrace him.

He rapped his fingers to the beat of Willie Nelson's "Winter Wonderland" and grinned.

"Let me snap a photo of you two." Sally grabbed her cell-phone. "Stand by the snowman."

Patrick fixed his arm around Cora, snuggled her closer, and they smiled for the flash of the camera.

On the return drive, Patrick repeated his thoughts aloud.

"I prefer this life compared to my prior one in Raleigh," he announced. "I'm no longer in the thick of world-shattering events, or off to interview a president or prime minister, or attend a swanky dinner with movers and shakers, and I couldn't be happier."

She met his sideways smile with a grin of her own. "Our one traffic-light communities suit you?"

"Budget friendly and slower pace. Loads of living space to sprawl out. The comfort of driving instead of relying on public transportation, and no sirens blaring in the middle of the night to wake me."

"Anything else?"

He glanced at her. "I love this ordinary way of living with an ordinary woman at my side."

"Ordinary?"

"Common people."

Her gaze narrowed. "As in average and unexceptional?"

"I didn't say that."

No reply.

For years, he'd prided himself on being articulate. He improvised spur of the moment comments on television with ease.

But now ...

Another pregnant pause.

"Cora, I—"

"Actually, you did say that." Her wounded tone scarcely hidden behind sarcasm, she murmured, "Thanks for clarifying how you honestly regard me."

When they crossed the town line for Evanville, he drew to the side of the road and held up his hands in regret. "You're not ordinary at all. I admire your traditional values."

Her face remained expressionless.

"You're valued and exquisite."

She wouldn't meet his stare.

This was worse than any outburst. Much worse.

"You're extraordinary, Cora." She made him feel strong, wise, and loved, but he couldn't find the words to tell her. He reached out to brush his fingers over her beautiful cheek.

She jerked back.

Her home was still a mile away. It could have been ten miles, because they drove the rest of the way in silence.

When they reached her driveway, he switched off his car.

Cora shoved open the passenger door and raced toward the house.

She spun as he followed her.

"Can we talk?" he asked.

"Sorry, Mr. Big Shot Anchorman, but this *ordinary* woman has *ordinary* things to do, beginning with laundry."

"Please. I didn't mean it that way."

"It sure sounded like it."

"May I explain?"

She shook her head. Her creamy complexion reddened. "Patrick, I'm pleased you found a better home for yourself here. However, I don't appreciate being categorized into a slot marked 'Plain Ordinary Woman' to round out your lifestyle."

He rubbed a hand over his face. "What I meant was how content—"

She stepped inside.

"It came out all wrong." He blew out an exasperated sigh. "Look, Cora. You're the best thing that has ever happened to me."

But he was explaining to a slammed front door.

CHAPTER SEVEN

*T*he following week was a brief one at the daycare.

On Wednesday, the children presented their annual program. Cora requested the parents and children to don their favorite holiday ugly sweater, and styles ranged from motorcycle-riding elves to sparkly blue unicorns. The youngsters sang three beloved Christmas carols, their voices bell-light and enthusiastic, their exuberance warming the audience's hearts.

Afterwards, appreciating the sugar cookies Cora had baked ahead of time, thrilled parents commented that their offspring sounded like a choir of heavenly angels, and wished Molly and Cora a joyous holiday.

"Christmas Eve is tomorrow," Molly reminded after everyone had left. "Your brother flew off to Nevada with his instructor and you ran the 5K. Cheers for raising money for a worthy cause."

"And Jack won the candy cane eating contest for the fourth year in a row," Cora added.

"He must still be on a sugar high," Molly said.

"My guess is he's recovering nicely. He's with Olivia, his pretty auburn-haired pilot instructor."

"Therefore, all's well that *might've* ended well." Molly cleared the toys and arranged them in a bin. "Agreed?"

"All's well that *ends* well," Cora corrected.

"Indeed?" Molly paused and scrutinized Cora's face. "This holiday ended well for you?"

Cora ignored Molly's insinuation. "Christmas is only two days away, so technically the holiday hasn't started yet. If you're referring to my disagreement with my father, we're having dinner together on Christmas Day at his house."

"A suitable beginning to mending your relationship."

In an accomplished issue change, Molly motioned to the floral bouquet on the kitchen table. Crimson carnations, holly berries, and frosted pinecones were designed in a white wicker basket tied with a pink velvet ribbon. "Where are all the candy canes I saw in there yesterday?" Molly peered into the basket and fished out a broken candy cane.

"I ate them," Cora replied flatly. "I'm becoming more and more like my brother because sugar is my current best friend."

"Why? Never mind, I'll answer my own question." Molly's expression empathized. "You're eating comfort foods because you miss him, right?"

No name. They both knew who.

"I miss him," Cora repeated.

A silent sadness swept through the room.

Lightly, Molly touched Cora's shoulder. "The flowers are beautiful."

"Gorgeous, but they're wilting." Cora offered a trembly smile. "I should discard them."

But she couldn't bear to.

"Who are they from?" Molly asked. "Patrick?"

"Yes."

"Any chance you're seeing him again?"

Cora shook her head. She couldn't voice any words save for a broken laugh.

He'd called. She hadn't acknowledged.

He'd texted. She'd deleted his texts without reading them.

It was better this way. A clean break with no regrets, no heartbreak. Perhaps in days or months, she would recover her equilibrium.

Why, then, were her lungs sore when she breathed, her arms heavy as if she carried a massive weight?

"Well, we're done cleaning." Molly shrugged a parka over her fuzzy penguin sweater. "I'm off to celebrate with Harry for our first Christmas together."

Cora shook off her self-pity and offered a heartfelt, "Bask in every precious minute and Merry Christmas."

"Merry Christmas." Molly dragged Cora close and patted her hair. "Hey, if you want to talk—"

"I'm fine." Through a blur of tears, Cora stared down at her reindeer sweater. "I'll manage. I always do."

*H*ours later, Cora sank onto the sofa with a cup of green tea and surveyed the two-foot "Charlie-Brown" tree she'd put up earlier that evening. Some might label the tree as pathetic—a skinny, two-foot tall fresh sapling.

For her, the tree symbolized the season. Real and authentic, trimmed with photo ornaments of the children she cared for. The tree reminded her of her peaceful childhood, before her parents had divorced and her father had hardened.

She grinned as she viewed the top of the tree, where she'd fixed an amusing ornament. A Scrooge that she'd found in town, complete with a pointed nose and narrow chin.

Patrick's handsome face flashed through her mind. He'd

referred to himself as Scrooge, except he didn't resemble Scrooge in looks or actions.

"*Bah, humbug*," he'd said. "*Perhaps there's a chance.*"

Was he truly so awful because of a statement he'd apologized for?

In fairness, no.

If weighing in impartially, though, then yes. For a journalist, he hadn't chosen his words wisely.

She blinked and gulped in a mouthful of air.

Their hours together had been wonderful—more than wonderful—for the couple of weeks it had lasted. She drank her tea and let the tears fall. Wasn't this typical for her—a brief connection that soon fell apart because she'd misjudged a man?

She set down her cup and went to stand by the window.

"'*To err is human; to forgive, divine,*'" he'd quoted. She remembered the fondness in his gaze, his tone a rich caress.

She recalled the day they'd first met, which must have been a difficult time for him. After packing and leaving everything behind in Raleigh—his career, his home, and his ex-wife —his elation at arriving in California had been dashed when his car had broken down. Yet, he'd been gracious and respectful and thankful of her efforts to help him.

None of it mattered now. Their situation commanded that she forget their pleasant hours together—his entertaining, lighthearted mannerisms, his romantic kisses and quips about the lack of mistletoe.

He was a man who smiled for the television camera.

And somehow, however feigned, she must learn to smile again too.

· · ·

*T*he dawn of Christmas Eve day brought guilt. In spite of her brother's good-natured teasing regarding a Christmas wish, she'd never actually thought of any.

In the afternoon, she attended a church service in Evanville, and then returned to her bungalow. While she wrapped a final gift, a miniature princess castle for Sally's daughter, Clarissa, her thoughts drifted back to the wish. She still had time to come up with one before her brother phoned on Christmas day.

Speaking of a phone, an alert on her cellphone made her pause. Molly had sent a link to the local television station and texted:

Watch the last five minutes. He's love-struck.

Who? Cora typed back.

You'll see.

Cora wavered. Since their disagreement, she hadn't watched Patrick's broadcasts.

Slightly unnerved, she opened the text. A video of the previous night's Bloomingfield news report began. Per Molly's instructions, Cora scrolled to the last five minutes and turned up the volume as the camera focused on Patrick behind the news desk. Her breath caught at how athletic he looked in a gray blazer emphasizing his broad shoulders, his forest-green shirt and an amusing Santa Claus tie.

He was concluding a weather-report chat with Lorenzo. His banter was concise and clever, yet elegantly all male.

"Before I take a few days off, I'd like to thank everyone for their guidance and good will," Patrick said. "Already, I've made friends with a number of people." The camera panned to a grinning Lorenzo who provided a thumbs-up, then swung back to Patrick. "I expect those friendships will last despite the fact I sometimes say incredibly stupid things. I sincerely hope I'll be forgiven."

Lorenzo took a seat beside Patrick. "Go on," he encouraged. "Anything else you want to say to the thousands who are watching?"

"Yes." Suddenly somber, Patrick's eyes welled with emotion. "There is nothing ordinary about this community. Merry Christmas to our entire viewing audience—including a very special woman who lives in Evanville."

Open-mouthed, Cora dropped onto a chair and stared at her cellphone screen.

Patrick was reaching out to her on live television. There was no trace of anything on his handsome, expressive face except sincerity. Thin lines of fatigue underscored his eyes. He looked drained, and she wondered if anyone besides her had noticed.

Her chest lightened. Her limbs relaxed. She took in a lengthy, shaky breath and brushed away unbidden tears.

Her Christmas wish had been apparent all along—ever since she'd met Patrick: a renewed attitude toward love and romance, and the ability to trust her own heart.

Laughing aloud, she phoned her father. "Dad?" she inquired quickly when he answered. "Merry Christmas Eve. A special man might accompany me tomorrow for dinner at your house. Is that okay? He's real, I promise."

"Do I know him?

She beamed. "In a way, you probably do. He's the new anchorman on our local station."

"Patrick Gervez?"

"Yes."

"Sure, I'd like to meet him. He seems like a great guy on TV."

"He's a great guy in person too."

"Does he know anything about cars?"

"Not a thing." She chuckled. "But he's an old car enthusiast, just like you."

Within fifteen minutes, Cora had changed into a silver sequined top and tweed wool skirt. She applied cream blusher in a berry shade, a touch of rosy lip gloss, and slipped on her four-inch heels. Instead of a headband, she clipped back her hair with a dazzling rhinestone barrette. At the last minute, she added gold translucent petal earrings for a dash of glamour.

She drew on her jacket, grabbed her gift for Clarissa, and headed to Bloomingfield for the buffet. She just hoped Patrick would be there.

*A*fter church services, which Patrick had attended with Oliver, Sally, and her daughter, he cruised directly to The Pasta Junction.

Upon arrival, scents of fragrant basil, garlic bread and olive oil prompted an appreciative sniff as he stepped in the doorway. Platters of antipasti with assorted cold meats and sharp cheeses, and a tempting display of dishes were set beneath warmers. Additional offerings included pasta carbonara, a creamy dish in which Julie's homemade fettuccini was the focal point, along with an array of flavorful stone-oven pizzas.

Holiday instrumental music strummed in the background, and Patrick wondered if Willie Nelson was on the playlist. Noting the restaurant's sophisticated ambiance, he doubted it.

"*Do you like the songs I selected?*" Cora had asked him when she'd chosen a medley of Willie Nelson tunes on their first date in the diner.

He hadn't liked holiday music. Hadn't liked anything that screamed *Christmas* since his divorce. But his mindset had changed, and he was embracing the season for how it was intended—a jubilant celebration, a positive attitude, and spiritual reflection.

Cora would be pleased.

Oh.

He recalled the inflection in her one word when he announced he wasn't a churchgoer, and the sadness that had crept into her voice.

After the church service that evening, he'd proclaimed to an elated Sally that he'd like to attend church every week, and had texted Cora to tell her as much. A glance at his cellphone displayed no response from her.

He sighed, signaled a passing waiter, and requested coffee.

"You'll be awake all night," Lorenzo wisecracked as he sauntered behind Julie, a tall slim blond woman, into the kitchen.

"I assure you, I won't," Patrick responded.

"This week has been chaotic." Lorenzo paused. "You must be as depleted as I am."

Patrick gave a curt nod, though sleep had eluded him the past several days, and the reason had nothing to do with work. Ever since his final conversation with Cora, he hadn't slept more than a few hours.

He scrolled to the photo Sally had sent of him and Cora in the diner. Aware he was tormenting himself, he enlarged the photo and ran a finger over Cora's cheek. She was smiling, her cheeks flushed. Her dark hair was a stark contrast against her white blouse and shiny earrings.

How was she spending Christmas Eve? Was she smiling?

He hoped so. She deserved to be happy.

"Cora," he murmured. "Please give me a chance to talk to you."

. . .

*W*ithin a half hour, Patrick was seated at one of several eight-foot tables, observing Lorenzo's twin nieces and Sally's daughter as they danced. Each of the little girls wore lace sweater dresses with knitted snowflakes around the hem, and he presumed the mothers had chosen the matching outfits for fun photos.

Sweet-smelling garland, entwined with snowy roses and clusters of wine-red berries, centered each table. Thick cream napkins were folded beside each emerald-green charger, and claret water goblets and sprigs of pine created a picture-perfect stage.

Cora would have loved this. She didn't care to cook, but adored dining out.

He grabbed his cellphone from the pocket of his navy blazer. It didn't hurt to try again, did it? If she replied, he'd happily volunteer to drive to Evanville, then back to the restaurant, although the distance involved might mean they'd miss the buffet entirely.

Maybe Julie offered takeout. He could buy dinner, then he and Cora could relish a cozy meal at her house.

If only she responded to him.

As he wondered how to phrase his latest text, he was dimly aware of the conversation from his nearest tablemates, Sally and Oliver. He absently replied to Oliver's question as he typed, *I miss you, Cora. Please let me make amends for my thoughtlessness.*

"Lorenzo's family is a jovial bunch," Oliver was saying. "His sister sent her daughter ahead so she and her husband could finish wrapping gifts from Santa."

Patrick picked a sprig of holly from the centerpiece and rolled it between his fingers. All that mattered was that Cora still cared about him, although he knew it was time to accept the circumstances. She wasn't interested in him anymore.

Sally got up, muttering something about helping Julie, leaving Oliver, who was commenting on ... Patrick didn't know what. He hadn't been listening.

Oliver studied Patrick with a perceptive grin and then glanced to the side. Lorenzo stood in the doorway and both men exchanged amused smirks.

"It's okay." Lorenzo clapped Patrick on the back. "We understand." With that, Lorenzo and Oliver started for the buffet line.

Patrick dragged out his cellphone, hoping against hope that Cora had answered.

She hadn't, and he shoved his phone back into his pocket.

Armed with a heaping plate of pasta, Oliver returned. "Any word from Cora?" he inquired casually. A bit too casually.

Patrick cut Oliver a dismissive glance. "As you well know, I haven't seen her since we ate dinner at your diner."

"A week without seeing the woman you love? It must be difficult for you both, especially at Christmastime."

"For her? Or for me?"

"She's obviously in love with you, judging by the way she looked at you while you were enjoying my mistletoe special," Oliver replied. "Is there a chance she's coming tonight? Sally mentioned ..."

The restaurant stilled, and Patrick stopped listening.

Slowly, he stood.

Cora had walked into the restaurant.

Her silver top and form-fitting skirt skimmed her trim figure, and high heels emphasized shapely legs and undeniable femininity. She scanned the tables, evidently searching for someone, clutching a wrapped gift embossed with reindeers.

Afraid to move, Patrick stood mesmerized for a moment, hearing her lilting laughter as she spoke with the hostess. Had she finally read his texts, his apologies, and appeared at last to talk to him in person?

He raced forward, and the overwhelming love for her made his throat ache. He disregarded the exchanged murmurs from the other diners.

"You're here." He stood inches away from Cora, almost touching. His gaze fixed on her beautiful face. "Why?"

"Because I couldn't face another tomorrow without you."

"I called. I texted. In fact, I just sent you another text."

"I haven't read it. I've been driving."

He opened his arms. She set down the gift and stepped into his embrace.

"You bought me a gift?" he asked.

"Not unless you like princess castles. It's for Clarissa." He loved her quiet laugh.

A burst of merriment from the children as they spun in a circle made him want to join them. This comfort and serenity only happened at Christmas, with the woman who meant more to him than anyone in the world in his arms.

"I must tell you some things." He took in a breath. "Many things."

"Right here? In the middle of the restaurant?"

"Yes. Beginning with, I'm sorry."

"I accept your apology. I realized you didn't intend to hurt me."

"And I love you," he continued. "Thank you for making my Christmas special by showing up here tonight. More than special."

Her gaze was warm and affectionate. "I love you too."

He glanced around. Plates in hand, friends and strangers alike were staring as Cora pressed a hand to his heart.

"I realized you are my Christmas wish," she said softly.

"And you're mine." He stroked his fingers over her face,

her lips. "You're all I want. You're all I want." He peered upward, hoping for a mistletoe.

Alas, nothing.

He bent his head and kissed her, gentle and loving. Who needed a mistletoe, anyway?

For the first time in forever, he'd found a town he could call home.

"A wish means you want something," he murmured.

She gazed up at him. "And that something is you?" Her smile was infectious. The same familiar smile that had brought gladness to his days.

"That something is us," he assured, kissing her again.

Because Cora Carpenter was his love, his happiness, and his Christmas wish.

The End

A NOTE FROM JOSIE

Dear Reader,

Thank you for reading *A Chocolate-Box Christmas Wish*.

I wanted to write another story centering around the characters in the "Chocolate-Box" series, and chose a character from a previous book, plus a new character—Cora and Patrick—to share a winter holiday romance with you.

If you loved this sweet romance as much as I loved writing it, please help other people find *A Chocolate-Box Christmas Wish* by posting your review.

The books in the Chocolate-Box Series include:

A Chocolate-Box Christmas- Love is sweeter with a touch of mischief.

A Chocolate-Box New Years- Fresh pasta isn't the only specialty that takes extra time.

A Chocolate-Box Valentine- It's your last love who truly matters.

A Chocolate-Box Summer Breeze- It's never too late to find love again.

A Chocolate-Box Christmas Wish- He's been all over the

world. She's a home-town girl. Can a holiday wish bridge the gap?

A Chocolate-Box Irish Wedding- Will their individual journeys lead them back to where it all began in beautiful Ireland?

A Chocolate-Box Christmas Wish is available in ebook, paperback, audiobook, Hardcover, and Large Print Paperback

I'd love to meet you in person someday, but in the meantime, all I can offer is a sincere and grateful thank you. Without your support, my books would not be possible.

As I write my next sweet or inspirational romance, remember this: Have you ever tried something you were afraid to try because it mattered so much to you? I did, when I started writing. Take the chance, and just do something you love.

My Spotify Play List for A Chocolate-Box Christmas Wish is here.

With sincere appreciation,
Josie Riviera

Love holiday romances? Grab all of my boxed sets:

Holiday Hearts Book Bundle Volume One
Holiday Hearts Book Bundle Volume Two
Holiday Hearts Book Bundle Volume Three
Holiday Hearts Book Bundle Volume Four
Holiday Hearts Book Bundle Volume Five

RECIPE FOR TARA'S CHURCH WINDOW COOKIES

Ingredients:

12 ounce package of chocolate chips
    1 stick butter
    1 package flaked coconut
    1 package colored miniature marshmallows
    1 cup chopped nuts (optional)

Directions:

Melt chocolate chips and butter in a saucepan. Let cool. Mix marshmallows and nuts (if desired) into chocolate when cool. Take a large piece of wax paper and sprinkle with flaked coconut. Spoon chocolate and marshmallow mixture onto the wax paper and roll into a log. Makes three logs. When sliced, the cookies look like church windows.

Chapter One

Colum O' Brien didn't believe in Ireland's much-heralded mythology. Aye, he was Irish to the core, but there wasn't a wee bit of truth to mischievous leprechauns guarding pots of gold. Gold buried by fairies, no less. Goaded by skeptical amusement, he shook his head. He didn't put much stock in ancient Irish folklore.

Which led him to another thought: Dreams. Did they mean anything?

In any event, he wasn't looking forward to sleeping in his childhood bedroom tonight. He wondered if he'd have the same dream that had plagued him for months on end.

Over and over, just before waking, he'd gotten lost while driving on a shadowy, winding road, never finding his destination no matter how hard he tried.

Well, that assuredly wouldn't happen on this trip.

With a dismissive smile, he switched on the car radio, humming along to the folksy acoustics of "Wild Mountain Thyme," a Scottish tune.

The weather proved fine and clear for an Irish December afternoon, soon to glow with the dregs of sunset before the sky turned blue black. He opened the car window a crack, inhaling the earthy fragrance of peat smoke mingling with the bracing air of the Irish Sea. He flicked a glance toward the neighboring hills, marveling at the flicker of twinkling white lights in cottage windows—heralding the holiday season— then returned his focus to the zigzag coastal road.

A sign noted the final turnoff to a precarious, narrow two-lane road. Soon, he'd reach his family homestead in Wexford.

Thirty years ago, Colum could have accomplished this drive from his former Dublin ballet studio with one eye closed, but not anymore. His fifty-year-old eyes didn't see as well as they once did.

Unexpectedly, heavy clouds began lowering over the surrounding hay pastures. Rain spattered his windshield.

He slowed his speed. It was as if he'd driven off into a different country with no recognizable landmarks. The sudden storm had even shut off his GPS.

Where was he?

The mist thickened. Road signs became unreadable. He lowered the volume on the radio.

Instinct told him he must be nearing the last tiny village on the outskirts of Wexford. Thankfully, the taillights of another car appeared ahead.

Perhaps a long-lost relative?

Colum's widowed father had insisted on a gathering at his seaside home for his wedding celebration and asked Colum to be the best man. His father was marrying a dear friend and set a December wedding.

At first, Colum had made excuses for not attending; he taught numerous dance classes, plus was helping Sean, a troubled young man in his twenties. Years earlier, he'd met the lad at a volunteer performance in Dublin. A feature story by an American newsman, Patrick Gervez, had spotlighted how Colum's ballet troupe had given back to the city by inviting underprivileged teens to watch free productions. Since then, he'd claimed Sean as his nephew, relocated him to Farthing, and helped whenever possible.

Thus, it was difficult to get away.

This trip was an eleventh-hour decision. Not that Colum didn't love his father—though in truth, he'd been resistant to return to Wexford. The longer time passed, the more he'd lost touch with his hometown. And whenever he drove these roads, his heart remembered Keira, his high school sweetheart.

Now it was her mother who would be his father's bride.

Would Keira be there? Wexford was the last place Colum had seen her several decades earlier. But no, she lived in London now, and his father would have mentioned her attending the wedding.

Perhaps. Perhaps not. He and his father didn't converse much.

The car ahead accelerated around a sharp curve, slid off the main road, then skidded to a stop on a gravel lane.

Colum's heartbeat slowed, his fingers tightened on the steering wheel. He stomped on the brakes and swerved onto the shoulder. Quickly shutting off the engine, he dashed from his car.

As suddenly as it started, the rain quit. The clouds thinned; then slunk away.

He dragged in a breath as the driver stepped out of the car.

A woman. A fair-skinned, willowy woman. And with her came a whisper of a memory: Their shared childhood and his love for her.

"Are you all right?" Anxiety brought a tremor to his voice. Fresh breezes cooled his heated cheeks.

"I'm brilliant." She peered at him with keen blue eyes. Blond hair, threaded with silver, tumbled down her back. The ends were tipped in . . . pink?

"Colum O'Brien. Is that you?" She touched a hand to her full, inviting lips—lips he well remembered.

He froze, his gaze fixed on her. He couldn't reply.

Keira Murphy. Here. He'd never expected to see her again.

End of Excerpt *A Chocolate-Box Irish Wedding* by Josie Riviera ***

Want more? Keep reading *A Chocolate-Box Irish Wedding*.

FREE on Kindle Unlimited!

Love the Chocolate-Box Series? Grab all the books here:

Or grab Chocolate-Box Double Hearts here.
All six "Chocolate-Box" books in 1 sweet bundle.

ABOUT THE AUTHOR

Josie Riviera is a *USA TODAY* bestselling author of contemporary, inspirational, and historical sweet romances that read like Hallmark movies. She lives in the Charlotte, NC, area with her wonderfully supportive husband. They share their home with an adorable shih tzu, who constantly needs grooming, and live in an old house forever needing renovations.

To receive my Newsletter and your free sweet romance novella ebook as a thank you gift, sign up HERE.

Become a member of my Read and Review VIP Facebook group for exclusive giveaways and FREE ARC's.

josieriviera.com/

ACKNOWLEDGMENTS

An appreciative thank you to my patient husband, Dave, and our three wonderful children.

ALSO BY JOSIE RIVIERA

Seeking Patience

Seeking Catherine (always Free!)

Seeking Fortune

Seeking Charity

Seeking Rachel

The Seeking Series

Oh Danny Boy

I Love You More

A Snowy White Christmas

A Portuguese Christmas

Holiday Hearts Book Bundle Volume One

Holiday Hearts Book Bundle Volume Two

Holiday Hearts Book Bundle Volume Three

Holiday Hearts Book Bundle Volume Four

Holiday Hearts Book Bundle Volume Five

Candleglow and Mistletoe

Maeve (Perfect Match)

A Love Song To Cherish

A Christmas To Cherish

A Valentine To Cherish

A Christmas Puppy To Cherish

A Homecoming To Cherish

A Summer To Cherish

Romance Stories To Cherish

Romance Stories To Cherish Volume Two

Cherished Hearts Six Book Volume

Aloha To Love

Sweet Peppermint Kisses

Valentine Hearts Boxed Set

1-800-CUPID

1-800-CHRISTMAS

1-800-IRELAND

1-800-SUMMER

1-800-NEW YEAR

The 1-800-Series Sweet Contemporary Romance Bundle

Irish Hearts Sweet Romance Bundle

Holly's Gift

A Chocolate-Box Christmas

A Chocolate-Box New Years

A Chocolate-Box Valentine

A Chocolate-Box Summer Breeze

A Chocolate-Box Christmas Wish

A Chocolate-Box Irish Wedding

Chocolate-Box Hearts

Chocolate-Box Hearts Volume Two

Chocolate-Box Double Hearts

Recipes From The Heart

Leading Hearts

New Year Hearts

SENIOR HEARTS

Summer Hearts

Christmas in the Air (1-800-Book)

A Very Christian Christmas

The 1-800-Series Volume Two

The 1-800-Series Complete

Christmas Tails of the Heart

Cocoa's Christmas Love

Pawfect Christmas Hearts

Pink Coral Island

Most books are available in ebook, audiobook, paperback, Large Print paperback and Hardcover.

Many are FREE on Kindle Unlimited!